MY FORBIDDEN Love

MY FORBIDDEN *Love*

A Soldier's Love Story

BELLE CHISHOLM

My Forbidden Love

Copyright © 2022 by Vera B. Akomah. All rights reserved.

No part of this publication may be reproduced, stored in a retrieval system or transmitted in any way by any means, electronic, mechanical, photocopy, recording or otherwise without the prior permission of the author except as provided by USA copyright law.

The opinions expressed by the author are not necessarily those of URLink Print and Media.

1603 Capitol Ave., Suite 310 Cheyenne, Wyoming USA 82001
1-888-980-6523 | admin@urlinkpublishing.com

URLink Print and Media is committed to excellence in the publishing industry.

Book design copyright © 2022 by URLink Print and Media. All rights reserved.

Published in the United States of America

Library of Congress Control Number: 2021925016
ISBN 978-1-68486-058-6 (Paperback)
ISBN 978-1-68486-059-3 (Hardback)
ISBN 978-1-68486-060-9 (Digital)

29.11.21

PROLOGUE

The clock went off at the usual time. I got up and went down to eat breakfast. Charmaine came down and asked if we heard anything from Pop's and his team. I told her nothing yet, but I'm going over for the morning brief with the COC if you want to go. She said, "Ooh, I'll just be in the way." "Well, you are welcome to come along, it's an open invitation," I offered.

Jai came in and asked, "Y'all ready? Tom called and said he's got some information on the mission." I asked, "Did he hear from Daniel?" She replied, "He'll fill us in when we get there." I asked Charmaine again, "Sure you don't wanna go?" She said, "No thanks, I'll stay here."

On the way to the car, Jai asked, "She's alright?" "She's just worried. I don't feel good about leaving her here alone. I'll have Soup keep an eye on her."

Everyone was there when we got to the COC. Tom said, "Come on in ladies, we're about to get started. We had contact with the coalition forces supporting Daniel and his team. They have gotten in and made the exchange on the hostages. The exchange was made near the borders and they're in route back if they do not run into any hostile resistance. I asked, "If there's a possibility of hostile resistance?" He replied, "Val, there's always a possibility of hostile resistance on that side of the world. Daniel is good at what he does because he knows how to react to any situation that may occur.

That's not my biggest concern; it's getting them across the border before the captors realize they just received counterfeit money from our government." I said, "You mean that was counterfeit money they used to pay the ransom, that sound pretty dangerous." He said, "But smart if they can pull this off.

I'll let Daniel explain it to you when he gets back, but what I will tell you, it was the federal government who, suggested the change in currency instead of Daniel using his own money as ransom. Yes, he insisted on being the courier. I don't have to tell you his reason for that. So all we can do now is play the waiting game and see what their next move. It may be hours before we hear anything from them.

I turned and looked at Jim and asked if there is anything you know of that could cause some delay in their getting to the border. He offered, "CSM knows the area better than anyone beside Chief. There are possibilities of Al Qaeda or the Taliban in the area and worse the weather could be their worse foe, especially if a sudden "Haboob" or sandstorm hit while they're trying to cross that rocky terrain. It gets really dangerous when there's no visibility. All we can do now is continue to wait for the reports to come in and hope for the best." I said, "Thanks Jim." I then walked out the room and stood at the wall and prayed that no one on this mission get placed on this wall.

Eloise came out and said, "Val, don't let all this worry you." I said, "I'm not worried, I was just praying." "I do a lot of that myself." I said, "I'm going to take a walk and try to clear my thoughts. I'll be back in a while."

As I walked out the building down the flight path my thoughts drifted back to when I first met this man who had made such a tremendous change in my life. I must have walked for hours.

CHAPTER

One

My thought carried me back to the EOC, when I first met Daniel. I could still feel the chill in the air as the fall seasons changed in the San Francisco Bay area.

Every year in November, the San Francisco Veteran's Memorial Opera House gave tickets to the military to attend the Opera at the Herbst Theatre. Formal attire, for the General's Staff, his Command Group and all Senior Officers were in attendance as their guest of honor in celebration of Veteran's Day. Sergeant Major Howard the National Guard Liaison to Sixth Army headquarters was the National Guard Representative. He asked me to be his guests.

Sergeant Major Howard, six foot tall, a very attractive dark skin black man, who's always sharp looking in his uniforms, and a nice body; if, I must say so myself.

He and Command Sergeant Major Douglas were always together. I would run into them when I would go to the NCO Club to get lunch. A couple of times I ate lunch with them. We would talk often when he came down to the EOC. He was married but his family was not on tour with him because it was a known possibility he would get deployed to the Gulf.

On this one occasion he asked me was I married; I said yes, very happily. He asked me was my husband here with me. I said no he's back in LA. He than asked, "Would it be inappropriate if I asked you to attend the Opera with me as your escort. I have to be there but, my family's isn't here either."

I told him let me get back with you because I don't have any dress blue's. He said, "Oh, that's alright you can wear a formal gown." I thought, oh great! Since I love to shop; this was the perfect time to go buy a new dress. He said, "The Opera is Friday night. I'll let you know the particulars." I said, "Ok, Sergeant Major."

I only had a few days to fine me a formal gown to wear to the opera. I was so excited. I had never been to one in my life. I did not know what to wear. I shopped for two days trying to find a gown. I tried on about ten different gowns. I finally came up with a navy blue straight tight fitting, flair bottom gown with black open toe "Payless heels". I felt it would match the Sergeant Major dress blue uniform.

Sergeant Major Howard came down the next day to give me the particulars. He said, since he lives in the same building I did he'll pick me up at five, we're supposed to have cocktails with the General at six in the "Green Room". The Opera starts at eight and then after the Opera we can have dinner if you feel up to it. I said, "Great, I'll see you than Sergeant Major."

He then said, "For the record my first name is "Daniel", so you can call me Daniel for this one time." "Ok, Sergeant Major." He laughed and said, "OK, Sergeant Acoma. See you Friday. Oh, by the way I'll be in "Dress Blues". I threw up my right thumb and said "Hoooah".

Friday I left work at noon to get ready for the Opera. Took a nap for a couple of hours and got up about three o'clock. I then, laid my dress, nylons and shoes and accessory out on my bed. I ran a hot bubble bath and soaked in my giant tub for about an hour. I washed and gel my hair and put it back in a tight bun.

My dress was a navy blue satin spaghetti strap body forming somewhat tight fitting with the flair at the ankles length of the dress; with zirconia diamond necklace and earrings. There was a chill in the air so I had a matching white satin shawl to throw around my shoulder and a matching satin navy evening bag.

Daniel arrived exactly on time. When I opened the door he said, "Sergeant Acoma, Wow! You look gorgeous." I said, "And you look handsomely sharp yourself, Sergeant Major." He gave me a soft kiss on the cheek and came in.

"First," he said, "Let's get some things straight. Can, I call you by your first name, which is_?" I said, "Yes, Valeria, but call me Val." "And you **will** call me by my first name, which is ?" And I said, "Daniel." Now that we got that straight are you ready? I replied, "Let me get my purse and shawl."

He stood in the living room and said, "You have a really nice place here." "Thanks to the compliments of the US Army." As I walked out the door he lightly touched my lower back for guidance as we walked to the elevator. *I thought to myself, this has got to be a dream and the night has just got started.*

When we arrived at the Performing Arts Center, it was dark at five o'clock. Command Sergeant Major Douglas and his wife were walking up the walkway. He looked stunning in his dress blues also. Command Sergeant Major Douglas' wife, who was a white woman, had on a black semi-formal chiffon dress. She looked very pretty. Command Sergeant Major Douglas did the introduction since he knew everyone. His wife's name was, Diane.

Daniel held my hand as we walked up the many steps to the Center. He continued to walk with his hand at my lower back as we entered the building. He was a pure gentleman. As we walked into the Arts Center it was like walking into a museum with wall tapestry lining the walls between the white columns along the long hallway. The floor was like glass marble with a gold carpet leading up the steps to the theatre.

We followed Command Sergeant Major Douglas and his wife down a long hallway that lead to the not so green room. The sign read, "The US Army Reception." As we walked into the gorgeously decorated room, there were officers and guests standing all around the room.

We followed Command Sergeant Major to the General's receiving line. As we walked through the line each person would introduce us to the next person in the line. When we got to the end of the line where

Lt General Harrison and his wife, introduction were made, and we were offered a glass of Champagne so the General could do the toast.

After all the toasts were made, the lights blinked several times for everyone to move towards the "Herbst Theatre". As we walked to the theatre I noticed how exquisite the interior of this building was. It was breath takingly beautiful.

All the military sat in the balcony with their guest as the "Special Guest" of the Herbst Theatre. We sat in the seats on the second row to right rear for a quick getaway if needed, but we stayed until the intermission. General Harrison and his wife sat in the box seat in the far left corner.

After dozing about three times I finally made it to the intermission of the program. We stayed until after the nine-thirty intermission. When everybody left to go back into the theatre for the second half of the program we decided to slip off, as many of the others did.

We followed Command Sergeant Major Douglas and his wife to the "Clift House Restaurant" that played Jazz music on Fridays. I ate a baked potato because I didn't want to feel or look tight in my dress. We sat and listened to the music on the dock until about midnight and the place started to get crowded from the late night party goers.

We left because I had duty the next day since I left early that day. Daniel took his military jacket off and put it around my shoulder. He said, "I know you are cold. I said, "Just a little chilly.

The fog was moving in quickly across the bay into the city by the time we had gotten back to the Towers. I told Daniel, "I had a wonderful evening and would he like a night cap?" He said, he had to turn in, because he was going in to the office tomorrow also.

But I'll take a rain check on that night cap. He gave me a soft kiss on my lips said, "Maybe I'll see you tomorrow." I said, "Well, you know where I'll be "down in the dungeon"." He then took his jacket from around my shoulders and left.

I walked out on the balcony from the living room that looks out on the city. I could see the fog rushing in from the marina had covered the streets. The lights slowly disappearing as the fog got dense until there was nothing but spots of lights showing down below. As I lean against the sliding doors *I thought to myself I really like this city with its dense fog and chilly nights.* I then went to bed.

Saturday at the Emergency Operation Center (EOC) was very slow. I was the only one on duty beside the Charge of Quarters (CQ) and the Staff Duty Officer (SDO) on Saturdays. I found myself catching up on the messages that came down from Department of the Army (DA). There were some National Guard units that were given their mobilization Warning Orders. People came by and asked how I liked the Opera. I told them it was really nice, I really enjoyed myself.

Sergeant Major Howard came down to tell me he really had a wonderful time last night, especially the presence of present company. I said, "Why thank you, Sergeant Major, I did too. He then asked, "If you don't have any plans, would you like to go out tonight?" Looking a bit confused I said, "Sure." He said, "I have an alert roster, I'll give you a call when I get off."

I found myself finding things to keep me busy. Command Sergeant Major Douglas came by to read the message log and asked me did I enjoy myself at the opera? I said, "I really did. It was the first time I've ever been to one. I have to admit I was kind of dozing there for a little while." He said, "Yeah, those things can put you to sleep after a while, especially after you had a few cocktails. I thought I caught the old man (General Harrison) nodding over there a couple of times."

He then said, "I just saw Howard leaving a few minutes ago. He said he enjoyed your company last night too. I said, "I'm glad he did." He then said, "Things are kind of slow around here today, why don't you close up shop. I don't think much going to happen between now and tomorrow. I just stopped to see has anything interesting happened. I'll see you Monday at PT Sergeant Acoma. Enjoy the remainder of your weekend." I said, "You too (Command Sergeant Major) CSM."

After Command Sergeant Major left I started to close up shop. I logged in the last of the DA messages and left for the day. I told the CQ, "If anything came up, call the Command Sergeant Major first, he has my number."

When I got home I heard my phone ringing. It was Christen, "My wife, how are you doing? I missed you so much." I said, "My husband I missed you too." We talked our usual about what's going on with the mobilization and Christen as usual, talked little about himself.

I told him, Sergeant Major told me that they may change my orders to mobilization order instead of Short Tour orders because its more advantageous to the government or should I say it would cost them less to house us here on tour. That means I would have to move out of this glamorous apartment into a smaller place and I may have to give up my rental car."

He said, "Well, let me know what's going to happen and we'll go from there." I told him, "I may get deployed also, depends on what comes up on the call up." He asked me, "Are you worried?" I said, "No, Not really, I always told myself since I joined the Army, if I have to die, let me die as a hero, that's not saying I'm going to die or want to be a hero".

He said, "I'll never let that happened. I'll kidnap you and take you to Nigeria." I said, "I could never make it there, no malls or nearby grocery stores." That made him laugh so hard. "Oh, my wife the avid shopper, you a soldier you can live anywhere."

"Yeah," I said, "but not forever, but just think, if anything happens, you will be a quarter of a million dollars richer." He then said, "My darling wife, money's not everything." I said, "That's coming from a Nigerian." He said, "No, from your husband who loves you very much." I said, "And I love you very much too.

I just got off and I'm going to take a shower. Call me tomorrow, but call me late, you know how I like to spend my Sunday's." He said, "Ok, I wish I was in there with you." I said, "I do too, I love my husband." He said and, "I Love you my wife" and we hung up.

I was just about to get in the shower when the phone rang again. I hesitated, about answering the phone. I was feeling a little guilty, about wanting to go out with Daniel, I answered the phone and he asked, "So, what you want to do tonight?" "Let's go to see a movie, "Back Draft" is playing up the street." "Great, let's catch the nine o'clock." "Great, I see you then."

Daniel called about eight and asked, "Are you ready?" "I'll meet you down in the lobby." We met in the lobby and walked over to the theater. The movie was over by ten-thirty. We walked around and looked in at some of the shops in the area. Daniel asked, "Since you're off Sundays, do you have any plans?" "No not really, why?"

"I was just thinking would you like to spend your Sunday with me, checking out the sights here in San Francisco?" I asked with a look of concern, "Why you want to do that?" "Val, I had a wonderful time with you last night, with the opera and the Jazz club and all. I'm just not ready to put an end to this weekend. Today I got my "Warning Orders" for deployment and I could be leaving soon for the desert."

"Daniel, you're married, and I'm happily married also, nothing can come of any of this." "I know; I just want to spend some time, with someone who I see as a very good friend. Who knows, what may happen when I get to that desert.

You know San Francisco is a very beautiful and Romantic city, if you take the time to really enjoy it. I've been here a year and I would love to show you the city of lights by the bay.

I can't think of a better way, to spend my Sunday than with you my friend." "Then, I would love to spend 'Sunday in San Francisco' with my new found friend." By then we were back at the Towers. I said Daniel, "You know where I live here in the building but, I don't know where you live." "Well, this is the perfect opportunity. I can show you where I live. I don't live in a luxury penthouse like you, only a regular apartment."

Daniel lived on the seventeenth floor in apartment 1706 not far from the elevator. "Would you like to come in?" "Not tonight," "I assume that means maybe another time." "Maybe." He then walked me up to the nineteenth floor to where I lived. He walked me to my door and opened my door for me. He winked and said, "I can't be too sure who may jump out here and grab you." I noted, "I'm a soldier, I'm pretty sure I can handle whoever may attempt something like that."

"I believe that, Staff Sergeant Acoma" as he gave me a soft kiss on my lips and left me standing in the door. He then said, "I'll call you in the morning, so we can get an early start on our day."

I closed my door, and as always I walked out on my balcony from my living room and watched the evening fog move slowly into the city below and said to myself, "What am I getting myself into, I hope it's nothing that I cannot handle." I then went to bed.

CHAPTER

Two

My phone rang early the next morning. It was Daniel, his deep sexy voice saying, "Good morning Sergeant Acoma get up and get dress, pick you up about seven-thirty in front of the building." I had already been up for about an hour. I usually get up early on Sundays and do my run on the Presidio trail along the coast. I told him, "I been up for about an hour." He said, "That's good, I'll meet you downstairs in a half hour, wear something comfortable."

I already had on a pair of white shorts and a red and white strip sleeveless top with white dock tennis shoes and a fisherman's wharf's pullover sweatshirt, because it gets chilly quickly along the marina.

I met Daniel in the lobby of our building. He had on a pair of kaki tan shorts and a tan short sleeve shirt. He said, "You look mighty comfortable." "I figure we might be doing a lot of walking today. You might need a jacket. You know how the temperature changes once the evening sun sets."

"Oh, we're planning on being out late?" I said, "I don't know, you tell me. So, where we're headed?" He said, "Sausalito for breakfast." "Great one of my favorite places, why don't we take my rental? You can drive."

We dropped the top on the mustang. As we drove across the Golden Gate towards Sausalito, we could see the sun slowly showed its big orange face as it edge its way just above the horizon. The sky around it turned a purple red. Once it reared its full round orange head above the horizon, the sky turned a bright orange. Daniel said, "Now that's what you would call a 'Tahiti Sun Rise' it's even more beautiful in the Caribbean's." "I can just imagine."

The Horizon Restaurant for breakfast was one of my favorite places for Sunday brunch. We arrived a little early for brunch. We sat outside the restaurant, as many others did who were also waiting for it to open. I told Daniel, "This how I usually spend my Sunday mornings, after my run on the trail."

Our turn came up and we told the waiter we wanted to sit, out on the dock. We had the waiter to bring us two mimosas (Champagne and orange juice) while we waited for our plates from the waiter. We ate a lite breakfast and walked off our meal and mimosa as we watched the village shops slowly open up. We stopped in at a couple of shops, where I bought a disposable camera. We decided to head back across the bridge into the city.

I said, "Since this is your Sunday in San Francisco, what are we going to do next?" "Well, my dear we're going to act like tourist. I've been here almost a year, and I've never been to 'Alcatraz' so there's a tour that leaves from the Wharf every two hours. So that's where we're headed now."

Sounding somewhat concerned I questioned, "So we're going on the water?" "Yes, is that a problem?" "That's one of the things I fear the most, is going on a boat in the middle of the ocean." "I swim very well, I won't let anything happen to my friend. So, what's the other, if this is one of them?" "Heights." He repeated "Heights! That can't be. You live on the twentieth floor of a high rise building surrounded by glass and wind that must get up to fifty miles an hour. I don't believe you."

"It's true, I took that apartment for many reasons, but the main reason was, because it was one of two left in the building when I got here. I was here during the earthquake, last October and I saw how hard it was locating bodies and people trapped in building that fell on top of them. I know it's a fact that the higher up you are, the quicker the rescue worker can get to you. So, my theory was, I have a better survival chance from my apartment than those in the apartments below me."

"So that's your philosophy, behind living in that penthouse apartment in the middle of one of the shakiest cities in the United States." "Well, at least I thought about it." "Yes, you did and it makes a lot of sense."

We parked in one of the parking lots near the wharf and walked down to Pier 41 to get tickets. It was about one in the afternoon by the time we got our turn to board.

Daniel mentioned as the wind picked up. "Are you alright? You might want to put on your sweat shirt since that wind start picking up." I did as he suggested. As we got closer to the dock of the island the currents start getting rough.

Daniel grabbed my arm and said, "I've got you." I mumbled, "My hero." He then caught my hand as we walked up the wet dock to the prison. We walked holding hands up to the prison gate.

On the tour, our tour guide showed us where Al Capone spent six years in prison and it is a myth that he died in prison of syphilis, but in his home in Florida of heart failure.

He said "The Bird Man of Alcatraz", Robert Stroud spent seventeen years in solitary confinement here before he was transferred to a Federal Prison hospital in Springfield, Missouri where it is said he died of his ailments.

He then concluded the mystery is no one saw him transferred and many believe he escaped from Alcatraz and swam the two miles icy bay and disappeared in the city. It is said he later died in Illinois and was buried there also.

There is no proof that a person can survive the icy waters of the San Francisco Bay and live to tell it. He said that's why it is said "the Bird Man's escape" is a myth or unfounded truth.

The tour lasted about an hour. When the boat left the island, it circled the island and headed north on the east side of the Bay towards the Golden Gate Bridge. Daniel moved closer to me and put his hands on my shoulders and asked, "Are you alright?" "I am now." The boat went under the bridge and turned and came back on the west side pass the Presidio.

It was the first time I had seen the post from the bay. I was amazed how much San Francisco looked like it was sitting on a big rock. The boat docked. I said, "I'm a little hungry let's get something to eat, like some Clam Chowder." He said, "Sounds great."

We found a nice little restaurant overlooking Fisherman's Wharf's main street where we could get Clam Chowder in a bread bowl. I asked, "So, what are we going to do next. He said, "I chose the first two things. It's still your turn." "Well, since we are down here, let's just walk around and check out the shops."

We walked from the south end of Fisherman Wharf to the north end. Daniel bought a sweat shirt. We then caught the trolley car back to where the car was parked. I said, "It's your term." "I was just thinking about that.

Since it's getting late, how would you like me to cook you a homemade Cajun dinner." I hesitated and said. "Cajun! So long as it's not too spicy. I had a bad experience with spicy food. Maybe I'll tell you that story one day." "Does that mean you want to see me again?" I said, "Maybe, so, what you going to make?" He said, "Shrimp and Pork Sausage Jambalaya. What kind of wine do you like?" "Mateus Rose, it's Portuguese." "I know, so we're having a Cajun meal with Portuguese wine. Seems like a nice combination.

We'll go by Whole Food and pick up some things and wine, then go to my place." "Why don't we cook and eat dinner at my place. I've been dying to use that gourmet kitchen for other than the microwave use."

We went to the store and got the things we needed for the Jambalaya. I paid for the wine, because I wanted to feel I was contributing something to the dinner. We went back to the apartment building. "Come to think of it, I don't know which apartment you live in." "Why pass up a great opportunity." He pushed seventeen. "This way I can kill two birds with one stone, and show you where I live and drop some things off. Just remember, I don't live in a glamorous place as yours."

His apartment was 1706. It was what I would called, typical Army. He gave me a grand tour and said, "You are always welcome in my humble abode." I said, "Thank you, the feeling is mutual. We then walked two floors up to my place.

I assisted Daniel in fixing the meal. I lit the candles over the fireplace Daniel poured the wine in the wine flute glasses. We then sat down at the dining room table. Daniel lifted his glass and said, Toast. "To a beautiful day with a beautiful classy lady" I lift my glass and said, "I thank you for sharing a beautiful day and evening with you, my friend."

It was silence for a while as we ate. I then said, "This is really good." "Not too spicy?" "No not at all." He then offered me some more wine. Silence fell on the table again. I asked him, "Would he like some more?" "No, thank you, maybe tomorrow but, let me help you with the dishes." "Oh no, don't worry about them. If I did those dishes my cleaning woman wouldn't have anything to do."

"You have a cleaning woman?" "She came with the apartment. She only does the kitchen and the bathrooms and, sometimes if I forget to make up my bed, but that's not too often." "I need to get some rest, you know we have mandatory PT formation, in the morning." "Oh, yeah you right it is Monday." He then said, "I want to thank you again, for a very lovely day." "It was your idea." He said, "But it still was, quite lovely.

We must do it again." "Maybe we will." I walked him to the door and he gave me a soft kiss on the lips and said, "Good night my lady, and get some rest." "And you too."

I then dimmed the lights and walked over to the living room balcony, and watched the fog slowly move into the city below. I closed the sliding door and said to myself, "I really had a beautiful day, one I will always remember, thank you Daniel Howard." I went to bed.

CHAPTER
Three

I woke up to my phone ringing. It was Sergeant Major Howard's voice. "Are you up" "I am now" "Just making sure, see you at formation." I rushed put on my PT clothes and took two B12's and dashed out the door.

I was running just a little late. When I got to the parade field parking lot, the first people I saw were Command Sergeant Major Douglas and Sergeant Major Howard talking. I walked passed and said "Good Morning Sergeant Majors". They both said "Good Morning Staff Sergeant Acoma" I said, Hooah and fell in formation.

I was so happy to know Staff Sergeant Jackson was giving PT. I did not have any energy for a long run or exercise. I guess everyone was trying to get over the weekend also. I had a Command Sergeant Major leaders' meeting every Monday morning. I went by the EOC to see did anything come into the office. There was a huge stack of DA messages and the new "Call up List". I made copies of the message and the Call up list for the Command Sergeant Major's meeting.

When I got to the meeting everyone was there except for Sergeant Major Howard. Command Sergeant Major Douglas announced, "There's a new DA message, I will read the part that will immediately affect this command and the EOC.

"The U.N. Security Council sent an ultimatum. It stipulated that if the Iraqi dictator Saddam Hussein did not remove his troops from

My Forbidden Love

Kuwait by January 15, 1991 a U.S. led coalition is authorized to drive them out."

He continued, "Things are about-to-get-hot. This means several things, and it affects the contingency support team also. There will be several changes effective immediately. The EOC will be on a twenty four hour work schedule; much similar to the one during the earthquake last year. There will be three rotating shifts.

The regular Army will support this mission until DA furnishes the funds to support and maintain the mobilization mission. Staff Sergeant Acoma will head Team One. Staff Sergeant Jackson will head Team two. You will be on a twelve hour duty schedule for the next few weeks. NCOICs will brief each shift change. Sergeant Acoma, I will get with you and your people on the other changes taking place later today." I said, "That's a Roger, Command Sergeant Major."

He continued, "Effective 1 December, DCST will be DCSOP. We will be Sixth Army Headquarter DCSOP. All operations and missions will fall under DCSOP. Many of you soldiers will be placed in mobilization status and many will be deployed to theater. So, I repeat myself and say things are "about-to-get-hot" and we are not talking about the weather. Staff Sergeant Acoma, I need you to have all your people in the EOC at 13:00 for a meeting with the Commanding General (CG)." I said, "Yes Command Sergeant Major."

After the leaders meeting I went home and took a shower, and changed into my BDUs. I went back to the EOC and informed everyone the Command Sergeant Major and Commanding General will be down to talk with us. Everyone was concerned, I said, "You'll know soon enough." I released everyone, "Go to lunch and be back at 1245. **Do not be late. I do not want anyone walking in when the CG is already here**, and I'll cover the front desk."

I had not seen Sergeant Major Howard since the PT formation. This was unusual for him, he's usually in and out the EOC often especially in the morning. I started reading over the recent stack of DA Messages on my desk and the distribution. I decided to look at the call up list, to see if Sergeant Major Howard's unit was on the list. There it was the 256th Infantry Brigade. He was assigned to an Ordnance Battalion.

I was so involved in what the list was saying I did not see Sergeant Major Howard standing at my desk. I heard a voice saying, "You're not eating lunch today?" "Maybe a late lunch, Sergeant Major. What can I do for you Sergeant Major?" He said in a low sexy voice, "If you only knew, I like to get a copy of that new call up list.

I understand my unit got its mobilization date." "Yeah Sergeant Major and it's a real close one too." I made him a copy and asked him, "You want to talk about it later?" "Sure, I'll give you a call when I get off." "Ok."

Command Sergeant Major Douglas came down, and reminded me, "Have all your people here before 13:00." "That's a Roger, Command Sergeant Major."

All the soldiers were back on time. They were asking what was going on and were they in trouble? I said, "No, but the Commanding General and the Command Sergeant Major needs to talk with us, I'm pretty sure it has to do with mobilization and deployment." Command Sergeant Major walked in just as I finished and said "ATTENTION"; we all stood up at attention. Lt General Harrison and Colonel Everett walked in and said "As you were people".

General Harrison pretty much told us everything Command Sergeant Major had told us in the leaders' meeting. He concluded and said, "Effective 1 December all of you will be placed on mobilization orders. There are some administrative things that need to take place and Colonel Everett and Command Sergeant Major Douglas will cover that." Command Sergeant Major called us to "ATTENTION" and the General left.

Colonel Everett informed us, "You all will be on mobilization order, which mean you will have to move out of the current housing you currently occupy. Those that are E4 and below will move into military enlisted barracks; E5 and above can either stay in post quarters or find a cheaper place in the area. I must warn you, your housing allowance will be much less than what you are currently receiving.

Some of you may eventually get deployed and if your home station is deployed you will deploy with that unit. Some of you may get deployed as filler to support other Regular Army or reserve unit. That is all I have right now, if you have any questions use your chain of command."

Daniel called me when I got home. He asked, "What are you doing?" "I just walked in the door." He asked, "Can we talk?" "Sure, just give me a chance to take a shower and change clothes." "I'll see you in about an hour." "Ok", and went to take my shower.

Daniel knocked shortly after I got dressed. I asked, "What's wrong, you sound so concerned. Did the Command Sergeant Major say anything about you and me?" "No! We're buds. We went to Sergeant Major Academy together. He knew I had my eyes on you since you got here." "So, what's up with the "I need to see you" all about?"

He said, "I just wanted to see you." "Well, is that all? You had me worried, that we were seen by some one." "Why, we were just friends enjoying the day together.

We did not show any affection for each other's in public, if we was seen." "I know I was more concerned for you than myself." "Just think I'll be gone in a few weeks and things will be back as they were. So, let's enjoy each other company until that happens." "Ok, but let's not be so obvious in the work place. Just call me when you get off from work.

I just recently had an enlisted female soldier who had a habit of being familiar with officers. I don't want that to happen to you or me." "So where do we go from here?" "I don't know, you tell me, we take each day at a time and enjoy each other's company." "I brought just the thing to help us stimulate this conversation." He had brought a bottle of "Mateus".

I said, "I know we both have obligations and commitments to someone else. So, we must be able, when the time comes to go our separate ways without any remorse."

We decided to walk over and get some cheese, and another bottle of wine before it got too late. Since it was a chilly evening, Daniel lit a fire in the fireplace and we sat and talked and drank our Mateus. Daniel opened the balcony sliding doors and asked, "Do you ever go out on your balcony?" "Sometimes, I like to look out on the fog as it moves into the city. It's spooky, but there's a beauty in that spookiness. I usually look out just before I go to bed at night."

Surprisingly he asked, "What do you sleep in, at night?" I asked, "What kind of question is that?" "After all, I am a man and it's only natural, that I would think of that, each night since we been together I thought about that when, I went to bed. So, answer my question." "Well, usually nude except on cold night, I wear a nightgown.

I like to feel the cold sheets against my body when I get under the covers." "That sounds sexy." "Now, that's not meant, as an invitation." "I didn't think it was but, I would like to know how long we're going to play this 'Cat and Mouse' game about our desires, for each other?"

"So, you have desires for me?" "Yes, and so do you for me." He continued, "But I have made my desires more obvious, by the way I touch the small of your back and among other small things, but you tend to ignore them.

I believe you are not one who is willing to get involved with someone sexually, other than your husband." I took a deep breath and said, "I just believe that, sex outside one's marriage lessens the value of one's relationship, with each other.

I've been married to my husband for five years and I have not had a desire for any man but him. I do not believe he's as faithful to our marriage as I am. I've had women call my house as well as come knock on my door, but it does not take away my faithfulness to our marriage. You know the old saying 'two wrongs don't make a right.' The sad thing about it is we have somewhat of an 'Open Marriage'.

My husband is Nigerian and we often have cultural disagreement, but they are only disagreement. I think he believes in this so called open relationship, so, he won't feel guilty about his infidelity.

That's why I'm always agreeing to go on assignment for the Army. I'm not a jealous woman, but nor am I stupid or any one's fool. There are the advantages for both parties. He's aware of those advantages also, even if we decide to split up, he may not divorce me because of the benefit he may lose out on.

You see, I know my husband, and he thinks he knows me better, than I know myself, maybe he does. We were friends in the beginning also, he wanted to get his citizenship so, he asked me to marry him. The sex was very good, so I said yes, even though I was not ready to get married. But now I am deeply in love with him.

So, as long as I continue to have somewhat of a single life and be married; we both can get what we want and be happy. He has not been here since I came on tour.

He's happy with his life back in LA and I love my life as somewhat of a freelance soldier. I know I can and will get deployed once the fighting start and I'm ready for whatever happens. So, what are you going to do for Thanksgiving holiday?"

"Are you trying to change the subject?" He asked. "Yes, I can see where this is heading. I plan to go home to Virginia. I haven't been there in a while." "I don't plan to go home, since my MOB date is so close, I plan to just stick around here and maybe catch a movie or something. I've never have been one for big meals." "What will your family say?" "They understand the situation and I told them, I'll make it up to them when I get back.

You see my dear. I've been married for over nineteen years to my high school sweet heart. We put a lot effort towards giving each other their space. We had our kids out of wedlock which was never an issue. The kids are both in college and they seem to have their own life now. I make good money as a Sergeant Major and she has everything she ever wanted, and I don't question it.

She knows I'm dedicated to the Army, and she wants no part of it. So, we're not so much as a happily married couple as it may seem. I asked her to come to San Francisco and go to the opera and she told me 'oh, that's boarding and it's not my style.' I didn't argue or made a big issue out of it. So, that's when my partner Command Sergeant Major Douglas, suggested I ask you.

I was taken back when you said, yes. When I came to pick you up and you open that door I was knocked, off my feet. You looked so beautiful. As a matter of fact "Tom" asked me is that Sergeant Acoma, in there? He said, man she looks very beautiful." "Well, thank him for me, he didn't tell me that, but he did mention how much you enjoyed my company."

"So getting back to my wife, she prefers just being Sergeant Major Howard's wife back at home. I told her I was getting deployed, and she asked what does that means. I told her that means I'm going where the war is. All she said was, "Oh." So, I'll make sure everything is in order before I leave and take some time to go see my kids before I deploy.

My son is in the ROTC at LSU, and my daughter is going to school in Maryland she wants to be a pediatrician. I'm going to fly out and see both probably next week. I'm really going to miss you those days." "Well take your time. I haven't really decided to go to Virginia for the holiday. Plus, I need to look for another apartment."

"Oh I heard something about that. Tom was telling me they were mobilizing the EOC soldiers to save money in the budget; which is understandable. So when are you going to start to look?" "Probably this weekend, I understand there are some nice ones over in Park City behind the Mall."

"Maybe I can help you go look." "I would love that. I'm going to miss this place when I leave. I was just getting used to having a place like this even though it was for only a few months; although it was a little over rated and priced."

"I hope you know Val, I want to spend as much time as I can with you before I leave. I know the Thanksgiving holiday is for family and friends and I'm not asking, but I hope you would spend it with me.

You know you didn't say anything about spending time with your husband in LA. What about him?" "Not sounding somewhat condescending, but he doesn't celebrate either of the holiday Thanksgiving or Christmas, that's why I usually go to Virginia.

He usually stays in LA with his friends. I may think about staying here. I'm sure my family won't mind considering all that's going on in the world. They don't understand the military either." He was sitting on the back of my sofa and bent down and gave me a kiss on my neck.

"I would really appreciate that my dear." He took me by the hand, and walked around the sofa to the front, of the sofa and the coffee table; and took my arms and put them around his neck, and said, "Now I got you"." He then gave me a very tender yet strong kiss. He looked down at me and said "Now that wasn't so hard was it?" I looked up at him and shook my head and said, "No." *(I thought to myself, Sergeant Major you are one hot brother).*

He then caught me by the hand and walked me towards my bedroom. He reached down and lightly turned the stereo up with "Kenny G" playing. I could feel the "Mateus" was working its magic. I said to myself as I took a deep breath, *"Finally."* I did not try to resist as I lay back on my bed and he kissed my neck and slowly started to undress me. At that moment I was all his.

CHAPTER

Four

I awoke when I heard the alarm go off. I was lying on my side and Daniel was laying on his side with his back to me. The alarm clock was on my right side of the bed.

He turned over and reached across me to cut the alarm off. He whispered in my ear "Good morning my lady" and snuggle close to me and I said, "And good morning to you," He pulled my covers off me and said, "It time to get up Staff Sergeant" "I know." "How you feel this morning?"

"Like a million bucks and you?" "Like two million." He kissed me on my forehead and whispered, "I like, the way you make me feel." "And I like, the way you made me feel, you got some skills there my friend." "I thought we've gotten past the friend part last night. Do I have to show you my hidden skills?" "Oh, there's more, in that case I'm all yours." We then made love again.

The brother had some moves. I did not want him to stop. I could not get enough of him. I said to myself, *if I had any idea what this man could do, I would have given it up days ago.*

We then got up and took a shower together. Daniel got dress quick and kissed me and patted me on my behind and said "See you in a little while" I said, "Hoooah, Sergeant Major."

I pulled out the parking garage and Daniel was right behind me. He blinked his headlights and I patted my brake lights. We followed each other onto the Presidio. When I got in the HQ building

Command Sergeant Major stopped me and said, "We should start the EOC scheduling shift on Monday. I need to get with you and Staff Sergeant Jackson sometime today." "Yes Command Sergeant Major."

When I got in the EOC, Sergeant Bigalowe told me we had gotten the mobilization order for people in this unit that's deploying. He put them on my desk. He said, "Our orders were there also for mobilization only with an effective date of 1 December." "That was quick."

I went to my desk to look over the mobilization orders that came in. They were arranged in alphabetical order by rank. I saw my orders and the rest of the EOC soldiers.

I continue to look through the stack and my heart sank when I ran across Sergeant Major Daniel J. Howard's orders with a mobilization date of 3 December. *I thought to myself "Damn" he doesn't have much time left here.* I made a copy of them and put a copy in his mail box at the front desk. I changed my mind and decided to carry a copy up to him.

He was standing in the hallway talking with Command Sergeant Major Douglas. I walked up the hall waving his orders at him. He said, "What's that - Mobilization Orders?" I shook my head up and down in motion of yes. I said, "I've got a present for you Sergeant Major." Command Sergeant Major asked, "What's the date?" I said, "3 December, in two weeks." He said, "Damn man, they're really trying to get you all there before the "storm"."

Command Sergeant Major said, "Sergeant Acoma, anything I should know other than I'm going to lose my National Guard Sergeant Major." "They cut the EOC mobilization orders for us." "That's good, what's your effective date?" "1 December." He asked, "You found an apartment yet?" I said, I've got some prospect to check out this weekend." "Let me know if you need some time to look and to move." "Hoooah, Command Sergeant Major."

I told myself I was not going to fall apart. It's not like I was in love with this guy. We do have a couple of weeks, and I'm definitely not going on leave to Virginia now. But I will take leave and stay in the area.

Daniel called and said, "He'll be over in about an hour." "I'm not going anywhere." "Want me to bring anything?" "You and Mateus in that order." "I heard that!" He knocked on the door about an hour later. He walked in and gave me a kiss on the lips and a pat on the behind. He asked, "How was your day?"

"A little stressful considering." "So you got your mobilization orders." "Um hum, and I've got to go to Camp Parks across, that Bay Bridge to my mobilization site to in process on the first of December. It's only a paper MOB since we are not getting deployed." "That's good." He poured me a glass of wine, and said, "Take this, it'll make you feel better.

I had a wonderful time last night. When I saw you coming up the hall this morning a certain part of my anatomy did an ATTENTION TO Orders." "You sick." "Like now, I want to pull those short off you and make love to you right here on the floor." "Slow your role Sergeant Major, I'm trying to eat my dinner."

He bent over and whispered in my ear, "My name is Daniel, or Dan not Sergeant Major. Don't you remember as many times you called it last night? You couldn't have forgotten it." "Oh, I remember, I remember very well." He bit my earlobe and said, "Well don't you forget it." This man had turned me on so much I could barely finish my jambalaya, but I did.

Just over night we had become more touchy feely in our relationship. He would massage my shoulder. "You decided what you're going to do for the holiday." "Yeah, I've decided not to go to Virginia or LA for Thanksgiving. But I do plan to take leave and stay in the area."

"That means we can have some full days to spend together." "I'm only taking a few days off and mainly to find an apartment." "That's good when does your leave start?" "Next Tuesday." "You gonna tell your husband?"

"Yeah, I'm taking the duty so my soldiers can take leave and go home for Thanksgiving, he'd understand. He's never questions what I tell him or shown me any signs of jealousy and I never question him. That's the substance of our relationship. I cannot remember us ever having an argument."

"I'm pretty sure, you'll think of something." He refilled my wine glass and hand it to me. He caught my other hand and said, "Come with me." We walked over to the sliding doors in the living room. As I stood looking out at the city, he came and stood behind me and put his arms tightly around my shoulder and said, "I love these times with you." "Be careful about using that word "love" it can get you in trouble."

"Ok, not to ruin the moment, I enjoy these times with you and I will always cherish them. They will give me something to hold in my heart when I'm in that desert." I smiled and said, "You are a Romantic!" "I don't know about all that, but I do know these have been some wonderful times, we spent together, I'm hoping you see it that way too." "I do."

We stood for a moment and watched the early fog moved in, as the lights disappeared leaving only a glow. "That is spooky, but it does have its beauty like you." He then kissed my neck. I said, "You know what that does to me? "Um hum, I know.

I think we should turn in early tonight, after all we do have PT in the morning." "You're ready to go?" "No not unless you want me to, but I do have to go to my apartment for a moment, and I'll be right back. So, don't fall to sleep." "Well take my other key," he kissed me on the neck and said, "That's to keep you awake." He grabbed the keys off the coffee table and gave me a wink.

The phone rang shortly after, I heard Christen voice say, "My wife, how are you?" "My husband where have you been you have not been answering the house phone?" "I know, but I got all your messages. (It never ceased to amaze me how he never had an excuse or gave me an explanation of his where about. I always felt I owed him one, even if it was just out of generosity, but he never asked for one from me).

So, you know I'm not going to Virginia for the holiday. I'm pulling duty so my soldiers can go on leave, instead." "My wife the Sergeant." "I'm pulling an eighteen hour on Thanksgiving, I got my mobilization orders and I will have to move out this penthouse apartment, so, I was going to look for one this weekend.

My, Sergeant Major was going to give me some time off. I'll let you know when I find one." "Sounds good, you sound a little tired." I had a couple of glasses of wine, I'm a little sleepy. I was about to get in the shower when the phone rang, plus I have PT in the morning. "Well, let me let you get some sleep. Maybe we can talk a little longer over the holiday." I said to myself, if I can find you. He said, "I'll call you" "Ok." We said our usual good byes and I love you.

I didn't know Daniel was back when I walked into the living room. He was standing on the balcony with the door closed. He said, "I didn't want to disturb you so I came out here, is everything alright?" "Yeah, he's just a hard person to fine when I need to."

He changed the subject and said, "I didn't know the wind was so loud and strong up this high." "It's like being in the clouds." "You right, I don't think I could handle that." "Did you do what you had to do?" "Yeah, I just had to make a call and pick up my PT clothes." He dangled my keys in front of him and hand them to me.

"I'm going to take a quick shower, so make yourself comfortable." "You take a shower before you go to bed?" "And when I get up except on PT days." "No wonder you smell so good all the time.

Is this a night you wear a nightgown?" "Only if you want me too." "Do I have a choice?" I hunched my shoulders. He said, "Why waste the time." So, I got in the shower and he got in with me and came up behind me and said, "I've always wanted to take a shower with you." "Is that what you really wanted to do?" "Yes, I want to be the one to wash you all over and rub you down." He tapped me on my behind and said, "So, hand me that body wash."

He got out the shower first and wrapped a towel around his waist. He went in the living room and came back with a two glasses of wine. I had gotten out the shower and was drying off. He hand me a glass and said, "Let me do that." I handed him the towel and body lotion. "Now my sweet lady, this is the part I really like.

Now, I want you to relax and don't tense up as I touch you. Lay back on your stomach. He squeezed the body lotion all over my back and slowly moved his hands massaging my shoulders to the small of my back. He squeezed lotion on my behind and slowly, but firmly, massaged it and my hips.

Moving slowly but firmly massaging down my inner thigh to my caves and heels; and then my foot and each of my toes. When he got to the ball of my foot he kissed the instep and did the same to my other leg and foot. As he firmly message me from the bottom of my feet back up to my shoulders he laid his famous, soft kiss on my thighs, butt cheeks, the small of my back and the nape of my neck.

He then whispered in my ear, "Val, are you still with me?" I moaned with an, "Um hum, but you almost lost me for a moment there." "Good, the best is yet to come. *(I thought to myself "Oh Shit")*.

He then turned me over on my back. "Now close your eyes but don't go to sleep because I know how to wake you up." "I won't." He took the lotion and squeezed it from my neck down the center of my body between my breasts to just below my belly button. He placed a drop on each of my breast and slowly but very gently massaged my shoulder and each breast. He continued to kiss each one as he move to his next spots.

He gently massaged my hips and sides moving towards my belly button. He then kissed just below my belly button. I twitched and he whispered "Move and you might miss something" I followed his commands and tried to not make a move.

He then put lotion on each of my thighs and kissed them softly massaging them very firmly and my shins and feet. He began to retrace the path he took on my body kissing all my sensitive spots. As he reached my breast he gave a kiss and nibble on each one. He then finally kissed my neck and ear and said softly, "Val, open your eyes babe and listen to me, follow my lead. All I want is to make you relax and feel good."

He continuously kissed me further below my belly button and below. I felt the inside of my body turn to melting butter. I did as he directed and follow as he was leading me to moments of deep sexual ecstasy.

We woke up with the alarm clock ringing at 0400. PT was at 0530. I grabbed a quick shower while Daniel got another half hour nap in. I felt tired so I took two B12 and a B6 to get some energy by the time I got to Presidio.

I woke Daniel up and told him it was time we got out of there if we were going to make it to PT on time. He told me to go and he'll be right behind me. I gave him a kiss and said, "I've got to go." He was getting up when I left. I left the extra set of keys on the kitchen counter with a note.

It was a good thing I took those vitamins considering the workout Sergeant First Class Brown had put us through that morning. I don't think I could handle it considering what my night was like. I did not see Sergeant Major Howard at the PT formation but it was Wednesday and it wasn't mandatory for him.

I was running the trail along the Point when I heard a familiar voice say "I really love that view from here" and another said, "Not bad, not bad at all". I stopped to get my breath and let the runners by. "Good morning Staff Sergeant Acoma." "Good Morning Command Sergeant Major and Sergeant Major." Command Sergeant Major asked, "You're alright Sergeant." "Hoooah Command Sergeant Major."

"You want us to wait for you." "No I got it." Sergeant Major Howard said, "You go on, Command Sergeant Major, I'll run with her back in" Command Sergeant Major ran ahead. He started running in place, I said, "I'm alright Sergeant Major, I was just trying to get my breath." Being sarcastic he said, "I thought maybe you were still suffering from last night." We started to run together.

I replied, "Me, you the one who couldn't get up this morning. I took, two B12's. I have a lot of energy, to burn." "Oh yeah, I meet you back at your place after PT. We'll see who has all the energy. Oh, by the way thanks for the key. I'll use it wisely." We ran back to the parade field together. He sprinted the last 100 meter. I decided to save my energy for, later.

When I got back to the penthouse, Daniel was already there, hiding behind the door when I walked in. "I told you, I'll use it wisely." He grabbed me around my waist and said, "Alright miss smarty put your money where your mouth is." "I got to get to work and, you too."

"No, I put my DA 31 in. I'm going on leave for the rest of the week. I was going to tell you later, but I decided to go visit my kids this week, that way you and I can have the last two weeks together before I leave for my mobilization site." "Oh that sounds good, when you leaving?" "Tomorrow, if I can get a flight but, I wanted to see you before I left; so how about a quickie?" "With you, it won't be a quickie."

"Well, you know I didn't get my breakfast this morning." "Well, I'm sorry you should had gotten up, when I got up this morning." "Well ok, you win this one, but I'm going to hold you to this when you get back tonight." "Ok, you can hold on to that key for a while." I went to get in the shower.

"Will you be here when I get back?" "I don't know, I'm going to pack some things and try to get some reservations. Maybe we can have a quiet dinner, before I leave." "Ok and gave him a kiss before he left."

Daniel called me at home, and told me he had some reservations for the next day. He had an early flight and Tom was taking him to the airport in the morning. He'll see me before he leave.

He came by the penthouse later that night. "I hated the thought of leaving, but there are some thing I needs to take care of now, in order for us to spend some time together before I deploy." He brought his bags up with him and said, "I hope you don't mind." "No why?"

"I didn't want you to think I was trying to infringe on you." "I know better." "I just wanted to see you before I left, and to hold you for a little while." We were standing in the middle of the living room floor holding each other by both hands. He took my hands and did a turn and put my back to his chest. We walked over to the sliding doors and looked out at the city. I laid my head back against his chest and said, "If it's this rough now, and you're only gone for a couple of days, I hate to think what it's going to be like, when you leave for deployment."

"Babe, don't even think about it, we have the next two weeks to spend together, and I won't let anything mess that up." "Me either, if I can help it." We kissed and made love right there on the floor in front of the fireplace. We sat up on the floor naked with the fire glowing on our face and just held each other tight.

Daniel said, "Set your alarm for two o'clock, Tom's picking me up at three, to catch a six o'clock flight. I told him I'll be standing outside waiting."

The alarm went off at exactly two o'clock, Daniel said, "Go get in the bed, under your cold sheets. I'll going to jump in the shower quickly. I won't wake you when I leave, but I'll take the keys if you don't mind?" He did as he said, I felt him kiss me on my forehead before he left. He reset the clock I fell back asleep until, I heard the alarm go off at five o'clock.

I heard my phone ring and it was Daniel. He said, "I was afraid your alarm wouldn't go off, so, I took some precautions. You did have somewhat of a disruptive evening. I hope you didn't mind?" I asked, what time's your flight?" "They're calling it now, I'll give you a call sometime tonight." "Ok."

Daniel called and said, he had a very good visit with his son Daniel. He was proud and concerned about my deployment. We just had dinner and I'm flying out tomorrow to see Danielle in Maryland.

He said after I leave Maryland I'm going to Seattle and see my wife. I need to make sure she understand what's about to happen. I should be back in San Francisco no later than Sunday, "I miss you and I think of you all the time." I said, "I miss you too." If he only knew! "You do what you have to do. I'll be here when you get back."

CHAPTER

Five

Daniel called me every night except for when he was in Seattle. I could understand why. He called me Sunday morning before he got on his flight and left me a message. "Baby, I'm coming home so, get ready." I wasn't in because I wanted to maintain the same schedule I had before I met Daniel. It was only an hour flight from Seattle.

When I got back to the apartment I cut on Kenny G. I always play Kenny because it made me think of Daniel. I went in my bedroom to take off my running clothes for my shower. I laid back on my bed and let the music take my thoughts. I must have dozed off because I didn't hear the apartment door opened. I heard a voice say "Hey Pretty Lady".

I opened my eyes and he was lying beside me with his head propped up on his hand looking down at me smiling. I said, "You're back." "No you're dreaming." "If I am I don't want to wake up." He then leaned over and gave me a big kiss. "I need to take a shower." "That's okI love it when you're sweaty." I roll out on my side of the bed and said, "Let me take a quick shower." "Well in that case, maybe I'll join you." We undress and he grabbed me by my arm and pulled me close to him and kissed both my breast. He then tapped me on my behind and said, "Hurry up." "I will, if you let me go."

We got in the shower together. He took the sponge and the body wash and said, "Let me do that, I missed your naked body so much," as he gently lathered my back and front. I turned facing him and tapped him on his nose leaving a soap bubble on it. I rinse the soap off me and got out of the shower. He said, "Did I say something wrong." "No I was just ready to get out the shower."

I was drying myself with a towel when Daniel got out of the shower. I said, "Let me help you with that." "I can do that." "I know but, I want to." I caught him by the hand and led him to the bed and said, "Now it's your turns, so lay down. I know you have had a long stressful trip. So, I figure you need to relax today." "Are you going to also?"

I put my finger on his lip and said, "Shh! don't say a word, I am in charge this time Sergeant Major." He said yes "**Sergeant**". I tapped him on his forehead and said turn over. I climbed my naked body over and straddle his lower back. I took the body lotion and squeezed a line of lotion from his neck down the middle of his back to where I was straddled.

I lean forward and gently massaged his neck and shoulders. He started to say something. I said, "Shh! Close your eyes and listen to Kenny. Think of only beautiful things. I gently massaged his back and waist line and slowly eased my hand down his lower back where I put a little pressure between his lower back and firm ass. I scooped down on his firm thighs and squeezed lotion on his firm ass.

I then massaged each tightly firmed cheek and bent down and kissed each one. (Man! he had a nice firm Ass) He twitched and I said "If you move, you might miss something" He smiled and said "You are so bad." "Shh!" I then slid completely off him on to the foot of the bed. I squeezed lotion on each of his tightly proportioned thighs.

As I massaged each inner thigh I kissed each one very lightly. He twitched each time and I gave him a tap on his behind. As I lotion and massage the back of his calves I noticed how tight and muscular they were. They were the legs of a runner and weight lifter. I massaged my way down to his heels, instep and the ball of his feet.

I gently massage each toe and slowly worked my way back up his body kissing each tender spot up to his neck and ear. He gave out a big sigh and said, "Hey babe." "Stay right there," as he turn on his back. He reached out his hand to touch me and I said, "No not yet." "You are so mean." "I just got started."

I asked would you like some wine. He asked, "Isn't it a little early?" "Not today, we're not going anywhere today. We're just going to stay here and enjoy each other's company." "In that case, yes please." He started to get up and I pushed him back down. "I'm not finished yet." He lied back on his back with his hands behind his head. I said, "Damn you look good." "You do too babe!"

I than straddle his stomach just across his belly button. I squeezed the lotion on his tight muscular chest. He then took the bottle from me and squeezed some on my breast and said, "I can't have all the fun." He gently massaged them as I massage his chest. He sat up with me in his lap and said, "Come here girl, I can't take this any longer especially where you're sitting!"

He grabbed me around my waist and turned me over and said, "Now you can follow my lead, now I'm in charge." He kissed my neck and then my breast. He then said with seriousness, I've never seen in him, "Val, I love you, I knew that the first time I made love to you." "You sure that wasn't lust," I interrupted. "That too, but I'm very serious.

I know you try to avoid using that expression, but I don't have a problem with it, when it comes to how, I feel about you. Babe, I'm not asking you to do anything you don't want to do.

I just want you to know, how I truly feel about you, and I love you." Daniel sat up and said, "Honey this is not a subject that needs to be discussed, it's just something I want you to be aware of. In a few weeks I'm going to be on another side of the world fighting a war we have no understanding of. But that has nothing to do with us. Does this mean I'm going to leave my wife, No? Does this mean you going to leave your husband, No?

But it does mean, believe it or not you can be in love with more than one person other than the one you are married to. Is it fair? Maybe not! Is it right? Maybe not! But, who are we to question it; when we knew from the beginning this could happen from the moment, we gave ourselves to each other.

So, when I say I love you; it does not mean I'm going to hurt anyone or destroy anyone's marriage. So, if that bothers you, I'm sorry honey, but I love you and I can't put it any other way. So now you know."

"So, what you expect from me?" "That's up to you, just because, I said I love you it does not mean you have an obligation to feel the same way. Although, I believe you do. Look honey the feelings you have for me is something you'll have to handle.

I cannot tell you what to do, to me it doesn't mean that your feelings for your husband is any less, or my feelings for my wife is any less. So, honey in my opinion, remember this is only my opinion; it's alright for you to love me and love your husband too.

People in other countries do it all the time, if I can remember you said your husband is Nigerian? Don't they have more than one wife?

I think you may already know this and may have also learned to accept it. But, it's alright honey just think you now have more than one person, who loves you. So, you now can love more than one person. It's alright honey! He leaned over and kissed me.

This was a little hard for me to take, but I could really see, where Daniel was coming from. I thought about those words for years. I think that is why I remain as Christen's wife to this day. I can be in love with someone else other than just my husband and still love him.

I remember his words "my darling wife a person can love someone else other than that one you are married to or significant other; but most cannot accept it, because most individuals are selfish with their love".

I thought out loud "Damn, why couldn't I have met you five years ago?" "Then you would probably be the one to get hurt. You're so vulnerable when it comes to your love, and it shows in the things you do and the way you care about your people in your section.

I can see why you are so hard, because you are a true crab. You protect your heart like it's all you have in the world, but that's what makes you vulnerable.

You know, what your husband is doing, but you justify it by saying he knows if he leaves you, he'll lose out on your benefits. What if he does leave you? I'll always be here in your heart and mind's. I'm telling you as your friend, and as your lover. Don't be a fool for anyone no matter if it's your husband or significant other.

You are such a wonderful person and you definitely deserve better." "What about you?" "I'm working on it. Maybe in ten years we'll meet under different circumstance, and we will be able to renew that love we shared here at the Presidio before the war; but it's almost impossible for that to happen. So my dear love, all we have is now and the next few weeks.

We both need to enjoy what we have now and cherish it forever." He laid down beside me and said, "Come here babe, let me hold you, so I can always remember how you feel." So we fell asleep holding each other close. We slept until noon.

CHAPTER

Six

When I woke up, Daniel had fixed brunch, omelets, strawberries, and Mimosa. I said, "It's time for brunch." "You did say we were going to relax, all day today." "Yes, you are correct." We ate breakfast in the nude at the breakfast nook.

I said, "You know you have a really nice body for a mature man." "Are you calling me old? I'm just forty." "No way, I'll be the last to say that, I'm just saying you do not have a beer belly and you have a nice firm muscular chest." "Well, let me tell you young lady," he said.

"As a Sergeant Major, I have to be in better shape than my soldiers. I usually do about 150 pushups and sit ups a day and lift weights as part of my fitness, you know this and of course, I run at least five miles a day. So, in order to continue to keep my body in shape and to maintain that physical endurance required for who know what is ahead for me, I must stay physically fit. So what do you do?

"I do sit ups some push up and I love to run but not five miles a day unless we do a battalion run. I do what I have to in order to pass the PT test. I used to do aerobics on Tuesdays and Thursdays but, that has changed in the past week." "Is that where you get those aerobic sexual moves?" "I don't know about all that, I thought I was doing as you said, following your lead; which means I was playing it by ear with a little ad lib in there also."

He came over and kissed me on my neck and shoulder, and said, "Whatever it is, I can't get enough of it." "Me either." I reached behind him and tapped him on his bare behind. He then said, "Come here babe." He took me by the hand and said, "Come here, I want to see something." I went over to where he was sitting and stood in front of him. "Take this leg and put it here on my leg. Now take the other and put it here."

I did as he said with his guidance. I was sitting on his legs facing him and he raised my behind up and placed me on his lap. He lean me back and kissed me on my neck and breast. I turned to butter and melted right there on the spot.

He whispered, "Honey, I just want you to see, and feel how much I love you and your body. I just can't get enough of you no matter what." He picked me up and said, "Now tell me babe, do you love me?" "Yes." "Then, tell me Val, tell me like you mean it, when I'm making love to you."

I said, "I love you, I love what you do to me and how you make me feel." "Now see, that wasn't so bad my darling. We both know how we really feel about each other, now that we got that all clear".

He carried me to the bedroom and we lied on the bed. I was no good for the rest of the day. We made love for the rest of the day until it got dark. We both fell asleep from exhaustion.

Daniel woke up first and hit me on my naked behind, and asked, are you hungry?" "No just tired, why?" "I was going to order a pizza." "A pizza, you Mr. Health nut." "Pizza, is an after sex food." "You order, and I'm going to jump in the shower." "Ok."

I took a shower and tidied up the bedroom. Daniel had cleaned the kitchen when I walked in. He looked at me and said, "Hey sexy, the pizza's here; you hungry?" "Yeah, I'm famished." I went and put on a tee shirt since Daniel had a towel wrapped around him. "You cold, I'll light the fireplace, I thought we're not wearing any clothes today?" "I was feeling a chill." "Come here babe, I'll warm you up."

"I was afraid of that." Daniel lit the fireplace and we sat on the floor in front and ate pizza and drank "Mateus". I asked, "Daniel, are you scared of going to the Gulf, with all the talk about biological chemicals?" "I thought about it, but scared no. I'm in an ordnance battalion and as a Sergeant Major with about four or maybe more companies, I won't have time to worry about me being afraid.

I would have about a thousand soldiers at the most to be concerned about. Me, I'm last on the list, it will be at most, my concern for all my soldiers. I have a responsibility to each one of those soldiers and they would expect that from me. No, I won't have time to even worry about what's going on back at home.

Val, that's why it's so important for me to leave with such positive thoughts, like the time I'm spending with you. This means so much to me, you just cannot imagine. When I leave here on the 2nd of December I will have a peace of mind, because of the time I've spent with you. You have played a huge part in that. That's why I can say, I love you.

"Well, you know I have PT in the morning, so I need to get some rest. When your leave ends?" "I'm on leave until the Monday after Thanksgiving. I haven't worked out since, the run we did before I left. So, I'm going in tomorrow and do some PT plus, I need to see Tom. So, if you ready to go to bed I'm ready." "You got your PT clothes?" "No, but I'll get them in the morning.

What are your plans?" "My leave starts Tuesday, and end on Monday, also. I'm going in also to make sure everything is covered on the days, I'm gone. Other than that, I was thinking about going to look for an apartment on Tuesday." "That's a good Idea. You want me to go with you?" "Sure, that'll be great." I then got up and went to the sliding door and stood and looked out on the city.

"It's a good thing no one can see up this high," as he walked over and stood behind me, and laid his chin on my head and said "I'm going to miss this view, also." "It is beautiful. It's going to be a late fog tonight." "I wasn't talking about the city or the fog. I was talking about you." "Oh" I turned around dropped his towel and laid my head on his chest and said, "Let's go to bed, I'm tired." He leaned over and locked the sliding door and said, "Let's go" and tapped me on my behind.

We lied down on the cold sheets. Daniel said, "These are some cold sheets." "Come here, honey, I'll warm you up." "That's ok I have a lot of body heat." I lied on his chest and said, "I wished this would never end." "I do also." I fell asleep on his chest.

The alarm went off on my side of the bed and I turn over and saw it was 4 o'clock. Daniel said, "It's time to get up. "I know." I got up, took two B12 and a B6 and got dressed. Daniel got up also and got dressed and said, "I'm going to the gym first. I'll meet you on the trail for the run. Do you take vitamins every day?" "Yeah if I don't forget it gives me that extra energy."

"Well save some for after PT, you may need it." "Maybe you should take some vitamins also; you've been a little slow getting up lately." "No I'm good." I kissed him and said, "I'll see you in a little while, you know I have the Command Sergeant Major Leader's meeting after PT." "Yeah, I'll be there."

I went by the EOC before I went to PT formation to see who was on leave. When I went out to formation, Sergeant Major Howard and Command Sergeant Major Douglas was standing in the rear of the formation. I fell in formation at the end of the rank. Sergeant Bigalowe gave exercise and had us fallout on a run on our own. I ran my usual route along the trail Command Sergeant Major and Sergeant Major came up behind.

Command Sergeant Major told Sergeant Major Howard, "I'll see y'all back at the meeting." I said, "I see you made it Sergeant Major." "I told you I'll meet you on the trail. So what's up Staff Sergeant Acoma?" "Same old same old."

He asked, "Am I running too fast, for you?" "No, but I don't want to slow your pace." "No, this is good. I need to do an easy run. I had a very vigorous day yesterday." "Oh yeah" He then started to speed up and said, "Meet you back at the meeting."

When I got back at the parade field everyone was back in formation. Sergeant Major Howard gave the safety brief because most of the soldiers were not going to be at Wednesday's PT because of leave for the Thanksgiving holiday. Sergeant Major reminded leaders of the Command Sergeant Major meeting and had Sergeant Bigalowe dismiss the formation.

Command Sergeant Major told everyone in the meeting that Friday is a holiday. The CQ will be in the EOC this weekend. All personnel going on leave will sign out through the EOC and sign back in through there also. Command Sergeant Major told everyone to have a good and safe holiday.

Daniel called and asked what we going to do the next few days. I said, "Well, Tomorrow after I've sign-out on leave, I'm going to look at a few apartment if you want to still go?" "Yeah that's great." I told him I got a call from a very close friend and she will be coming up on Wednesday to spend Thanksgiving. "That's good. Then we could have a dinner after all." "We can talk about it later."

Jackie Taylor had become a very good friend. We worked on a couple of exercises together. She was assigned to the Support Command Materiel Management Center. The unit was the Support Command's subordinate unit that supported the command for all the equipment needed to support any mission assigned to the Corp's Support Command.

Jackie was a dark skin beautiful black lady. She was a little stocky but damn good at what she did. Jackie was a woman of the world. She was a Sergeant First Class and had been in the Army Reserves awhile. Jackie held several MOS and one of the critical MOS needed for this deployment.

She called me and said she came up on the call up list as a Movement Control NCO. Her job was supervising the movement of freight, cargo, personal property, and passenger travel at the installation level. As a supervisor she serves as the transportation liaison representative between other military services, commercial agencies, and host nation support elements. She was deploying November 30.

I invited her up to spend the holiday because she was leaving in a few days and she was willing to bring some of my personal stuff up when she came up. I told her, "I'm moving because I was mobilizing also. I needed some things if she could bring them up when she came." She said, No problem, that way she could drive her van."

Daniel said, "I'll pick you up early and we can get some breakfast. I'll give you a call when I'm ready." Daniel came over later and slid in the bed beside me. He said, "I couldn't stay away from you tonight, I just wanted to lay here beside you and hold you. I said, "Ok," and fell asleep.

I woke up with the phone ringing. It was Jackie. She said, "I got your boxes from your apartment here in LA. I'm going to leave and probably be there tomorrow morning. I'm on leave for the next few days and I'm going apartment hunting today. I told her be careful and I should be back home by the time she get there."

Daniel and I ate breakfast at an IHOP near the shopping mall and the Park City apartment complex. I really wasn't in the mood to look for an apartment. I was suffering from withdrawals of moving out of the Penthouse.

"Babe, you're going to be alright." "I know, I was just having too much fun especially since I met you. I rented a two bedroom apartment with a balcony and a fireplace. It had a small kitchen, with a nice view. I decided to move in at the end of the month. That way, I did not have to pay the Towers any money.

"The Towers cost me $200 a day; where this apartment would only cost me $900.00 a month. I wrote a check for three months of rent.

We went and looked at some furniture for the new place. I wrote a check for $2,000.00 worth of new furniture, I thought at least I'll own it. Since, the government owed me for my final month of TDY; which would be about $8,000.00."

Daniel mentioned, "You should be getting a nice little chunk from your TDY money if you move out the Penthouse. Why don't you buy a "Hoopdee" to get you back and forth to work? Then you won't have that rental car to worry about or getting a ride to and from work. I'll help you find one. We can do that after the holiday." I said, "You're so good for me." "I know I love you too." *(He sound like Christen)*

Tom and Diane invited us over for Thanksgiving dinner. *I thought to myself I am not ready for this.* I asked, "Do you think we should cook something for Thanksgiving?" "You know, we are not ones to do a lot of cooking, it might just be a waste. We can go and pick up some things at the grocery like some cheese, strawberries and Mateus." "That sounds good."

When we got back to my place the phone was ringing. It was Jackie. She said she was not coming up until Saturday. She had some things to take care of. I said, "Ok, just give me a call when you get on the road." I hung up and told Daniel my friend Jackie won't be coming up until Saturday. He said, "I guess that means we can go to Tom and Diane's for Thanksgiving dinner." I said with a deep sigh, "I guess so." "Hey babe, it's going to be alright."

He then said, "I know what's wrong, you still have a problem with people seeing us together. Honey, whether you know it or not people have already seen us together, beginning with the Opera. If you think it was an issue your Command Sergeant Major would have said something to both you and me. So don't worry your pretty little head about such matter.

If you think this was a problem, don't you think Tom would have said something weeks ago and would he invite us both as a couple to Thanksgiving dinner." I said, "I hear you. I just don't want either of us put in an uncomfortable position."

"Don't worry babe, I've got your back. Just look at it this way, in about a week everything will be back to normal, you running the EOC, and me Sergeant Major of some battalion, out in the middle of the Saudi Arabian desert."

He then said, "Who knows, you might just enjoy yourself." He walked over to the sliding doors where I was standing and handed me a glass of Mateus. He then stood behind me and kissed me on the top of my head. He questioned, "Only these moments."

I said, "No not only these moments, but I just feel there is something deep when two people have times together other than making love or sex they can reflect on, gives a true meaning of their relationship. I am going to miss you so much. Everything about you; your smell, your taste, your deep voice; and most of all, the way you comfort me when we are alone.

I just feel this is straight out of a movie and I get to play the role as the leading lady; and you get to play the leading man. Who would believe it all began "A night at the Opera"." He leaned over and kissed my neck.

He then looked up and said, "The fog is moving in early tonight. From now on when I see fog I will always think of you for as long as I live. I know it's going to be very hard for both of us when I leave on deployment, but just think we have some beautiful memories.

Who knows for all you know Sergeant Major Howard may shed a tear or two, but it will only be because I fell in love with a woman I can never have for my own. I love you and you love me, so let's not end in sad good byes. We're both soldiers with a mission.

You will have other lovers, as I may also, but we shall always remember our love before the "Desert Storm"." He then sat his empty glass on the end table and put both arms around my shoulder and said, "Staff Sergeant Valeria Acoma" thank you, for giving me the most beautiful three weeks a soldier could have before going to war." He then whispered in my ear "I Love You". I said "I Love you too." He said, "Let's go to bed." We then walked to my bedroom with both his hands on my shoulder.

The alarm went off at six o'clock. Daniel reached over on my side of the bed and pushed the button. He said, "Let's go run over on Post. I need to work up a hearty appetite for that Thanksgiving dinner, you feel like a little PT this morning?" "Sure, I could do for a run today."

We rode over to the parade field and jogged over to the scenic trail. We ran the two miles trail and down to the marina and back. It took us an hour and a half for the complete run. On our way back we ran into the local San Franciscans doing their annual "Turkey Run" along the Marina.

We decided to go by Whole Food and get some champagne and orange juice and go back to the apartment and make some Mimosas. Daniel made cheese omelets and I made the mimosas. We sat and watched some of the annual Macy's Parade on TV. I was a little exhausted from the four mile run and the mimosa so I laid across the bed for a quick nap. Daniel came in and laid beside me and said, "You mind a little company?" I said, "Sure."

The phone rang, it was Christens' voice, "My darling wife, Happy Thanksgiving." I got up and walked into the living room. I said, "Same to you, my darling husband, I was just thinking about you." He said,

"I thought you were on duty today." "I am, I got the twelve to twelve shift, I got a few minutes before I get dress.

I found an apartment over in Park City. It's close to the airport. It's a two bedroom with a fireplace. It's not the penthouse but looks comfortable and its only $900.00 a month.

He said, "That sound great. I'm thinking about moving out of this area up into the North Hollywood area. "That way you can save some money. I think I found one." I asked, "Is that what you want to do." "It's more to both our advantages when it comes to finances." "Well, if that's what you want.

Jackie's coming up on Saturday maybe you can send the rest of my clothes up by her that way if you have to put stuff in a storage you won't have to worry about mine's." "That's no problem you can keep them down here."

"There's a possibility I will get deployed soon myself, not by the Support Command but by Sixth Army." "Well, let me know what's up then." "I will." "When you going to move?" "Maybe next week, I'm really going to miss this penthouse lifestyle." "I'm sure you will."

"It's a shame you didn't make it up here, to see it." "I know maybe next time." "I've got to go take a shower so I won't be late for duty. Call me tomorrow. I'll try to get in touch with Jackie and see if she can swing by and pick up my other clothes."

"If that's what you want." "Let me know, if you need anything. I love you and miss you so much." "I love you and miss you too." We then hung up.

Daniel was lying on the bed sleeping like a baby when I went back in the room. I lied down beside him. He asked, "Is everything alright?" "Yeah same as always." "That doesn't sound good." "I know."

He turned over and put his arms around me and said, "Things are not always as bad as we sometimes think it is." "I know I love you too." He kissed my neck and we made love. We then fell asleep and woke up about one o'clock. Daniel called Command Sergeant Major and asked what we need to bring Command Sergeant Major replied just bring some wine, we have everything else.

Daniel said, "Ok see you in a little bit." When we got to Command Sergeant Major's house it was around three o'clock. I assisted Diane in the kitchen doing the finishes on the dinner. Command Sergeant Major and Daniel were in the den watching the annual Dallas Cowboys and Washington Redskins play football.

Command Sergeant Major's three sons were there also. It got really loud each time a favorite team made a touchdown. (This brought back memories during my ex-husband's family annual Thanksgiving dinner but less stressful) Diane set a standard rule once the game is over dinner is served.

Command Sergeant Major said, "Once I get home I have no authority. Diane runs everything and I do as she tells me." I said to *myself Sergeant Major's wives are like General's wives, they really do think they wear the rank also.*

Thanksgiving holiday tradition always includes the game of "Spades" the favorite card game of the military past time. Daniel and I were partners against Command Sergeant Major and Diane. We end up beating everyone who sat down to play. We decided it was time to go after winning so many games.

As we walked to the door Command Sergeant Major asked Daniel when he starts out processing. Daniel replied, "Tuesday's my last working day, I have some things I need to do some closure on. I'll be in and out the office during those days." Command Sergeant Major then asked me, "Have you found a place yet?" I told him Command Sergeant Major. He insisted, "You can leave off the "Command Sergeant Major." I replied, "Yes, over in Park City." He then asked, "When you plan to move?" "Sometime next week before the first of December."

"Why don't you take a couple days pass for Monday and Tuesday and let me know if you need an extra day, otherwise I'll see the both of you on Wednesday." I said, "Thank you Command Sergeant Major." He turned his head to the side and looked at me.

When we got back to my place, Daniel said, "I have to go to my place and do some things I'll be back shortly. So don't go to sleep, you know I know how to wake you up." "I know you do." When he left I poured a glass of Mateus and walked over to the sliding balcony door. The fog was coming in fast. I said to the fog, "I'm going to miss this nightly ritual of seeing you come into the city." I raised my glass and said to you "fog" set my glass on the end table and went to bed. I climbed in bed between my cold sheets as it touched my body.

I must have dozed off when I felt Daniel's naked body moved close to my backside and kissed the nape of my neck. He asked, "Babe you sleep?" I turned over and laid in his arms and said, "I'm not now." "I just want you to know, I love you very much." "I love you, very much too." We fell asleep holding each other tight.

The alarm went off on my side of the bed. Daniel reached over and hit the off button. He said, "Come on babe, let's go run." "I'm too tired to run." He said, "No you not, Staff Sergeant. I need some motivation. Here take your B12, it'll give you energy." I got up put on a pair of sweat and took my B12s. He said, "We'll do a short run today, down the marina and back to the post HQ." "Ok, but don't try to push me on the run."

By the time we got on post my B12 had kicked in. I had a lot of energy. We ran the Marina and back. Daniel did not have to push me. Daniel said, "I need to go by my office first." "That's good, I'll sign back in from leave," so I can take my pass on Monday.

I went to the EOC to sign-in off leave. Sat around and read some of the DA messages that came down. Daniel called and asked, "Have you been to the Wine country?" "Yes, when I was down at Camp Roberts. It's not far from there." "How far is it?" "About a four hour drive down the five. It's really nice. I liked it a lot."

"I have some tickets, I need to use before I deploy. Let's go today, and make a day of it." "That's if it didn't get burnt out, during the Painted Cave fires that burned down Santa Barbara." Well, it's a nice fall day, for a drive. We'll go change clothes and leave about ten o'clock." "Ok, I'll meet you at the car."

We left about ten thirty. It was a really nice autumn day and the weather was really warm. We had sweat on just in case the weather changed on us. We took Daniel's rental with the sun roof.

When we got near Camp Roberts you could still smell the burnt out soot in the area. As we passed the area where the road was scorched by the fire, I told Daniel about the night the fire burned on both sides of the road, as we drove through the fire on this highway to evacuate the fire victims.

I told him, "I was more scared at that time, than during the San Francisco earthquake. A twenty foot wall of fire on both sides of the highway and smoke covered the roads with no visibility. I thought we were really going to die that night."

Daniel looked around on each side of the road as we drove down the highway. He said, "Oh my God, this place looks like it was burnt to hell." "I thought I was in hell. I prayed the whole time, but watch this, just as we turned the next bend; there is no trace of fire only a burnt tree here and there.

I have to believe it was because of my praying and the others on the vehicle." "I don't believe what I see. This has got to be a miracle. You were in the middle of all this." "Yes, me and a convoy of soldiers with goggles and wet kerchiefs around our face to keep us from choking to death. I have to say by God's grace, is how we made it through it." "I'm glad, just think or I would never have met you.

And all this just happened a few months ago?" "Yeah back in June." "You are a very lucky young lady, to have been through the middle of a forest fire, that destroyed a town and before then the earthquake that almost destroyed a major city." "Not lucky honey, just blessed and it will all be a part of my memoirs someday." "That's some beginning."

We went to a wine tasting at the Hearst's Castle off, Pacific Coast Highway. I told him, "I know of a very quaint little seaside town called Morro Bay that has the best seafood." He asked, "Shall we go?" "If you feel like eating seafood. I know a nice restaurant that overlooks the bay where we can have a nice candlelight dinner.

There's a favorite spot near a cove, where I used to go and watch seals and their pups come in on the beach and play amongst themselves." He suggested, "We can drive by there, and then have dinner at that quaint little restaurant."

We went down on Seal Cove. We sat on the rocks and watched the seal pups play and tussle on the beach along the rocks. The adult seals standing guard as they played. If anyone moves towards the pups the adult seals would prance in their direction to protect them.

I told Daniel, "This is where the adult seals bring their pups out of harm's way of sharks that feeds on the pups. This is a safe haven for the pups until they're weaned from their mother, and then they're on their own.

When I was here there were a few seal pups that let human come near them because they would feed them fish, but the fish and game officer stop them because they said they needed to learn to hunt their own food or they will die during the winter months. Otherwise, the fish and game officers from department of water and games, would have to feed them during the winter months to keep them alive."

As he looked out over the ocean he said, "You know a lot about these little guys." "I told you this was one of my favorite spots. I had a friend who used to work here for the water and game commissioner. I would come here on my day off and just sit and watch the pups play for hours and then drive back across the mountain to Camp Roberts. Plus I am an animals' advocate.

My favorites are dogs and cats. I prefer dogs more than cats or people, especially when I was a little girl." He asked, "Why is that so?" "Because dogs are more loyal and faithful, they would go to any length and are very protective towards those who love and care for them. All they want from you is to show you love and care about them."

The sun was beginning to set out over the ocean. I climbed down the rock from where I was sitting between Daniel's legs. It was breathtaking as the sun slowly moved downwards towards the ocean. As I stood on the cove along the beach, Daniel came up behind me and put his arms around my shoulders and said, "I can see why you like this place so much." I said, "Beside the pups, it's the sunsets that stole my heart."

The sun was like a big orange ball slowly slipping into the edge of the ocean. Daniel said, "What a beautiful sight, especially with the silhouette of the seals swimming in the water. It is a picture to remember." We stood on the shore and watched the day slip away from us, as the tide rolled in and the sound of the bell and the fog horn in the distant.

Daniel then said, "Let's get something to eat." As the sun disappeared in the water, we walked along the beach with his arm around my shoulder and mine around his waist. He said, "This was a beautiful day." "It's not over yet." "You're so right."

When we got to the "Gaslight Restaurant" there was a line, but short. Daniel gave the maître d' our name and asked how long would it be. The maître d' said, "About thirty minutes." We walked the board walk along the pier and listen to the fog horn in the distance. Daniel said, "The fog must be coming in."

"There is an old lighthouse just down the beach to warn fishermen of the rough water along the shore. It's still manned by the department of fishing and game. When the fog moves in you can see the light beams showing through the fog. Many people are scared of the fog. I just have so much respect for it, since I moved into my penthouse. That's because the fog never rise above my floor. I am otherwise looking down on the fog and not inside it looking out." "That's a good observation."

We walked back to the restaurant and the matre'd told us our table will be ready in five minutes. We looked at the menu on the wall and decided what we wanted to eat. We sat at a table by the window overlooking the bay harbor. Daniel ordered a Carafe of white Chablis, lobster for him and the large fantail shrimp for me. The waiter poured our wine.

The very low yellow glow of the lamp on the table set the ambiance of a very romantic atmosphere. Daniel picked up his glass and said, "To memories that will never be forgotten." We drank a sip and I said, "To a romance that shall never be forgotten, you've stolen my heart." He then gave me a wink. We took another sip and we held each other's hands and rub them gently. "I wish this would never end." He said, "It never will in our hearts." I smiled and pat the back of his hand.

The waiter brought us our huge meal; a big lobster that hung over Daniel's plate and more shrimps than I could count. We ate in silence and made comments about how well the meal tasted.

An older white couple walked past our table and stopped and excused their selves and said, "You two look so in love." Daniel wiped his mouth and said, "We are, thank you sir." The old gentleman said, "I knew it, I could see the glow in both of your faces." He patted Daniel on the shoulder and said, "Good luck and don't ever lose that feeling." I said, "That was sweet. He must be a romantic." We ate the remainder of what we could eat and asked the waiter for a "To Go" bag.

I asked, "You ready to head back." "I guess so it's been a long but, beautiful day. One I will always cherish. If you get sleepy just lay the seat back. I'll wake you when we get back." I laid the seat back to rest my eyes. I felt Daniel hand on my thighs. I then put my hand on his and we rode the way back to San Francisco with hands on each other's thighs.

I heard a voice say, "Babe we're here." "Already!" "You awake." I asked, "I slept the whole way?" "Yep, you sure did, but "Kenny G" and 'Frankie Beverly" kept me company." We went up to my place. I pulled all my clothes off and threw them in the chair in the bedroom and flopped on the bed. Daniel told me to get under the covers, he'll be right back.

I later felt Daniel climb in bed beside me and slide his naked body up against mine. I said, "There's my man." He turned me over and said, "We're right here waiting for you." I felt him slide inside of me and I was no good. I said, "What a way to end a beautiful day." He kissed my neck and I melted.

The alarm went off as usual. Daniel reached over and cut the alarm off. He said, "Come on Staff Sergeant, it's time to get up and do some PT." "PT, I'm on leave." He said, "No you're not, you signed back in yesterday, or did you forget." "That's right, but it's Saturday." Daniel said, "So, get dress; take your B12s and let's get going." I said, "Ok, ok." "I need to go by my place first. I'll be right back." I got up put my sweats on, took two B12 and lied back on the bed. Daniel called "I'm ready, meet you down stairs."

We ran the marina from the post to the marina and back. My B12s kicked in and I was good to go. We stopped by the Whole Foods and picked up some fruit and went back to my place. The thing about B12s, it gives you a temporary boost of energy and when it's over you are down for the count. When we got back to the apartment I was really exhausted. I lied on the living room sofa and dozed off to sleep. Daniel was stretched out on the loveseat with his legs hanging on the floor. We were both knocked out.

The phone rang and it was Jackie, said she was just passing Camp Roberts and she should be in San Francisco in about three hours. I said, "Just call when you get close to the City. I'm going to the store what do you like to drink? She said some wine or maybe some "Kahlua" I said, "Kahlua" what's that? Daniel said, "I know, I got it."

When Jackie got close to the City I had Daniel to tell her how to get to Presidio. We would go and have her follow us back to the Towers. I was so happy to see her. I formally introduced her to Daniel as a very close friend who is also getting deployed in a few days.

I had Daniel put Jackie's things in the second bedroom on the other side of the apartment. I had it already made up for any overnight guests. I let Jackie get settled in from her long ride. She loved the penthouse apartment. As always I would say compliment of the U.S. Army.

Daniel went down to his apartment while we girls did some catching up. He said he had to do some things down in his place but I knew better.

Jackie said, "Ok Val, I've been dying to ask you. Who is the tall dark and handsome? Tell me everything and don't leave out a thing." "Well he's National Guard and AGR. He's married with a set of twins in college and his wife doesn't like the military but loves the fact he makes good money. We've been lovers since he took me to the Opera, three weeks ago. He's deploying December 3rd as an Ordnance Sergeant Major. That's pretty much it.

Jackie said, "The Opera Val, and a Sergeant Major. He looks mighty young for a Sergeant Major. All the ones we know are old with one foot in the grave." I laughed and said, "I know he's forty, but it was something that just happened. He invited me to the annual Veteran's Opera, at the Herbst Theater and we started spending time together almost every day after that. "He's been a real gentleman and been there for me. We both are married and we just enjoy each other's company.

We just love being together and spending time together and it has been a hot and steamy relationship. Yesterday we spent a very beautiful day in Wine Country and had a very romantic dinner at the Gaslight Restaurant in Morro Bay. He's a romantic and we enjoy each other's company. So, that's enough about me and Daniel."

I then asked, "So what's going on at the Support Command?" "Same old-same old, Sergeant Mashon is still working in your office. I think Mr. Morey has a thing for her. Everybody is up in the air about possibility of war. They have set up a 24 hour EOC." "It's about time, if Sixth Army HQ has one its down traces should also. Who knows I may be on that deployment list, soon myself.

Daniel walked in and said, "You ladies still trying to catch up. He walked over and kissed me on the top of my head. I pat his hand. He asked, "So what you two going to do tomorrow?" "I'm going shopping, for my new apartment at the mall or maybe a little sightseeing." Jackie said, "Yeah that's a good idea." Daniel said, "While you ladies are out, that'll give me time to do some things myself."

Daniel went down to Jackie's van and brought up my boxes she had gotten from Christen. We drank wine and the three of us talked to the midnight hour. Jackie said, she was going to turn in she was a little tired from her drive. She told everyone goodnight and went to her room. I went over and stood by the sliding door and said, "Here she comes." Daniel asked, "Who?"

"The fog. She moves in like a cheating female and slips away in the morning light. She sometimes lingers during the day, not wanting to leave, but by noon she's usually gone until night falls again." Daniel said, "That sounds very poetic and beautiful," as he came over and stood behind me. He then kissed me on my neck and said, "I'm a little tired let's go to bed." "You go on, I'll be there in a moment."

I just wanted to watch the fog for a while. I watched the double lights moving together in the fog. As I turned around, I saw Jackie was standing in the kitchen. She said, "I didn't want to disturb you. You looked like you were in deep thought." "This is a nightly ritual for me to stand here and watch the fog move in each night, and then I go to bed.

Jackie asked, "Where is Daniel, now?" "In bed, our plan is to spend every night together until he leaves. Jackie, I really love Daniel. It's going to be hard for me when he leave. Although we only been together for about three weeks. Those weeks have been a life time for me. I have never been this happy ever in a relationship. Not even with Christen, and he's my husband and I love him. I doubt if that's still the same. But that's another story for another time.

It's hard to let that someone go that you love; but it's that much harder when both of you are so much in love with each other. You see Jackie, I know Daniel loves me very much, and I love him. We've talked about our love for each other a lot." Jackie said, "Wow, Val that's deep." I said I know it's so deep I don't want to let him go. I don't know. I'll just have to wait and see. I better go to bed before he wondered where I am. We'll talk more about it tomorrow when we go shopping. I then said, "Good night" and went to my bedroom.

Daniel was awake when I got out the shower. He asked, "Are you alright, babe?" "Um hm." "I heard your conversation out there, I wasn't eavesdropping even though, you both were whispering. I could still hear a good portion of the conversation."

He sat up in bed and said, "Come here babe, I don't want to hurt you, when I leave." "I know it hurts more now, as the time gets closer to your leaving." "Who knows, you might end up over there some day yourself, and if you do. I will find you." "I believe that, too." "Now come here, and make love to your, other husband, like you never did before." And I did.

Daniel got up before I did and went to do his usual thing his morning run on Post. He told me he'll be back soon. He was going to meet Tom on post and they were going for a run.

Jackie and I got up early and just hung out. We went to a place in Sausalito for Brunch. I only drank one mimosa. Jackie had two. I told her, "Daniel heard our conversation last night, he wasn't upset but he was very concerned. I think he was more concerned than he let on.

You see he's usually getting me out the bed. These last few days to go running with him, but this morning was different. He said, he was going to meet Tom who is our Command Sergeant Major, and go run this morning. They haven't hung out together since the Opera. I think he's having a hard time with this departure, as I am." She said, "I'm sure he is too.

What I have noticed, when I see you two together I can see the love you two have for each other. But, just remember girlfriend, you have a life and a husband back in LA." "I know, you're right." We went and checked out some of the shops. I suggested we go check out my other place at the "Fisherman's Wharf".

I told Jackie, "I think Christen is involved with someone or ones back in LA." "Why you think that?" "Well, for number one, he's Nigerian and from what I know, from living in DC they believe in having many sexual partners. Then, I can never find him at home, when I call and it takes him days to return my calls. Even though he sound happy to hear from me, he never gives any explanation or excuse why it took so long to return my calls.

So, when he told me he wanted to give up our place in West LA and move to North Hollywood, I think he is trying to separate and not say it. If he is, maybe it's for the best." We then walked around and brought some souvenirs and later went to do some shopping at the Park City Mall.

On our way back I showed Jackie where my new apartment was. She asked, "Are you planning on staying here in San Francisco?" "I hadn't planned to, I don't know, but I do like it here. I've gotten used to earthquakes. I think I'll stick around here until maybe I get deployed."

She suggested, "Why not put in a mobilization packet? You can get picked up quicker." She said, "That's what I did. You have more than one MOS." I said, "Yeah." I can give you my contact and you can send your packet through him." "Thanks, I appreciate that."

When we got back to the penthouse, Daniel was there watching the football game. I asked, "Did you and the Command Sergeant Major have a good run?" He said, "Yeah, we did a real good one. Did y'all enjoy yourselves today?" I said, "Yes, we did a lot of catching up." He said, "That's good, you hungry?" "Not really, you know I still have those shrimps from our trip the other day." He said, "Oh, that's right." "Order some Chinese food."

Daniel ordered the Chinese. I ate my shrimp and they ate Chinese. Jackie said, "I'm going to leave early tomorrow morning." I said, "Not, so soon?' She said, I'm mobilizing on Sunday, I need to finish packing." I said, "I enjoyed your company, I just wish you could stay longer." She said, "Maybe next time." She said, "I'll call and get you that information."

We sat and talked a long time before she decided to go to bed so she could get up early. I asked, did she want me to wake her; she said, "Not really, but if you didn't mind setting your clock for four o'clock?" "That's the time we usually get up for PT, on Mondays." I checked to see if the clock was set for four. I then stood and watched the fog come in and Daniel as usual came over and stood behind me and kissed my neck. He handed me my glass of Mateus.

I asked, "How was your run with Tom?" "We talked, I told him I'm in love with you; he said he figured that. He asked me, what I'm going to do, I told him I don't know, all I know is, I love her, man. He asked you going to let it fade away?

I told Tom we talked about it, but that's about it. We'll just let it play its course and see what happens. He said, you both can get hurt behind this. He said we need to just break it off. I asked him is that your opinion. He said, No just a friendly suggestion.

He said you both are in the same situation. What you both are doing is against regulation. It is known as adultery and infraction. Both are Court Martial offenses. You only have a few days left. Just don't let your good byes be messy. Then I have to get in it. I told him we won't let that happen. He said Ok man I'm counting on you to do the right thing. Don't leave her in a bad condition. Love can be very painful if you are trying to end a relationship."

I said, "Maybe he's right." Daniel said, "He is right, but I can't do that, we both are in too deep. You see, when I leave, we will go our separate ways. We just need to stop thinking and talking about it. We'll just enjoy each other's company, knowing when the end will come."

I said, "When I look at you I will stop saying to myself, he will be gone soon. I need to just enjoy the moment." He said, "Now that's my girl." He caught my hand and walked me to the bedroom. We went to bed and made love. And I will continue to count the days.

The alarm went off as usual at four o'clock. I got up to wake Jackie. She was already up and dressed. She said, she had been up since three. She wanted to get on the road by four. She said, she really enjoyed herself and she was going to call me when she got back, with that information. I said, "Please I would, appreciate it." We walked her to her van. I gave her a big hug and told her to follow the sign to south on the five. Daniel gave her a hug and said, "We enjoyed your company." She said, "Who knows, I might see you over in the desert." He told her, "Maybe soldier, drive carefully."

CHAPTER
Seven

As we walked back to the elevator, Daniel asked, "You want to start moving things over to the new place?" "Not really. I wasn't in a big hurry to move yet. We can do it tomorrow. They are delivering the furniture tomorrow." "It's still early, I'm going over to the office and clean up a few things and when I get back maybe you'll feel like doing something." "Ok" He got off on his floor, and I continued up to my floor.

I couldn't get out of my mind what, Tom had said to Daniel. I said to myself, why when I find a really good man he always has ties, to someone else or married. (I was referring to Donnell) I said, "I know it's wrong, but I have no regrets."

When Daniel got back I was packing things, I had brought for the penthouse to take to the new apartment. He asked, "You feel like doing anything?" "Not really, I thought, maybe we just hang out here and just do nothing. I still have a few personal things I want to pack." "Can I help?" "You can pack the things in the living room, and if you have any questions just ask me,"

There is something, I've been meaning to ask, but did not know how." "What is it? I'm a big girl I can handle it." "You said you've been married about five years. How come you don't have any kids, or if you do, you've never mentioned them?"

I was standing by the fireplace and said, "I can't have any more children. Funny thing, that's the first time I've been able to say that.

He came over and put his arms around me and hugged me really tight. He said, "Oh, babe I'm so sorry. I can see this is very hard on you. Please forgive me for asking."

I said, "This is something that happened a life time ago. I sat on the arm of the sofa with my feet on the cushion seat and said, "I'm forty years old, and I've gotten over not having children." "You don't have to tell me what happen." "But I want to.

You see, I was married once before I met my husband, Christen. I was married for about ten years to a guy I went to high school with, after I joined the Army; whom had a lot of personal issue, he couldn't handle, but instead took it out on me.

He had a lot of anger which he had too much pride to try and get help. He blamed me for everything that went wrong in our marriage. For a long time I had lost all my self-esteem and the will to defend myself. He had a lot of affairs throughout our so called marriage.

He carried me through a lot of verbal, mental and physical abuse in our ten years together. I got out the Army because he felt the military was no place for women, even though I loved being in the Army."

Daniel said, "I know you did, look at you now. He got up from sitting on the other end of the sofa and asked, you want a glass of Mateus?" "Yes please." He gave me the glass and said, "Go on I didn't mean to interrupt you."

I sipped the wine and said, "So, I got pregnant, unfortunately it was one of those many times that he hurt me so bad it caused me to miscarriage. I had to go to the hospital. Well, I had to have a hysterectomy.

One day while visiting my mother-in-law she told me she did not want to wake up one day and find out that her son had killed me.

I later found out he was still married to his first wife. This was an even more motivation to get away from him, but it had to be well planned, a smooth transition.

I had a good job with the federal government, working for the Department of the Army with a "SI-Top Secret clearance". Part of that duty, I ran courier to the Pentagon and the White House which was 100 miles away. I put in for transfers. I eventually got lucky and was offered a job working for the Chief of Staff of the Army on the "D" ring at the Pentagon.

I worked for a COL William Westmoreland one of the Assistant Chiefs of Staff (ACofS) to the Vice Chief of Staff of the Army (VCSA), who is probably retired now, but was a two star last I heard. He worked for the VCSA, Lt General Maxwell Thurman the now TRADOC Commanding General. I worked for them for over three years, until I remarried and came out to Los Angeles, and the rest is history. So, now you know."

Daniel said, "Now, I know why you are who you are. What life has dealt you! Everything happens for a reason. Just think of what you been through these last two years with the forest fires and earthquake, you are one strong woman. You handle crisis very well." I said, "No, I don't, I pray a lot and they have gotten me through some tough times. So remember that, while you running around in that desert." "You right, I will."

Daniel went to the kitchen and held up the empty bottle of Mateus, and said, "I'll run to the store and get some wine." "Pick up some cheese while you're there."

After Daniel left, I thought to myself I have been through a lot in these past years. I'm blessed, because I could have been killed many times back in that house on Paige Street. My family and friends afraid to get involved because of his family's reputation in sticking up for each other.

Daniel came in the apartment, he opened the Mateus and brought me a glass. He asked, "You alright?" I said, "Yeah." "He then apologized, "I'm sorry, I forced you to open old wounds. As I looked in your eyes as you told me all that happen. I saw how you tear up when you tried to explain certain parts." I said, "You too my Sergeant Major, it was hard recalling that period in my life. It's all behind me now."

Daniel then said, "You know when you told me about how he kept you away from friends and relative, and you were from a small town. I wouldn't normally say anything, but I believe he did that to keep his secret of still being married. He didn't want anyone to tell you the truth.

Especially after you married him and carried his last name. He knew his family wasn't going to tell you because of their bond and family ties. So, he would rather put you through hell in order to not let you find out the truth that he was nothing but a selfish, weak, egotistical womanizing bigamist. It had to have been killing him trying to keep that lie from you."

"You know I can only imagine it's hard living a lie when there are so many who knew the truth; to be in fear that the truth would come out one day. I was so weak and scared at that time of him. I met Chris who showed me what love and companionship was like. He gave me a freedom I never knew exist in a relationship. I owe him so much. He was my friend.

When my friend told me he needed a favor from his dear friend. He needed to get married. He didn't know at that time I had already fallen in love with him. I said yes. He changed my life and showed me what true love, marriage and happiness was all about. I owe him so much. And then I met you Sargent Major. One day I will write my life story and it will be worth reading.

"You know honey, I knew there was a reason I met you. You put a lot of light on that whole time he carried me through that tormented life with him. You summed it all up in just a few minutes. I thought it was because he came from an abusive family environment, and because he was just hateful but it was more than that. I actually believe my love would make a difference, but it didn't.

He was living a lie but didn't want me to find out through my friends and co-workers. He succeeded for almost ten years. I was a total mess until I moved to DC on my own and found the person whom I lost and who I really was."

He said, "Well, in that case the doctor's office is closed for the remainder of the day." He reached down and pulled me up off the sofa and said, "Come here babe." He rubbed his hands up and down my arms and said, "I wished things were different for us. I would spend the rest of my life just giving you the love and attention you so royally deserve.

But it's now, I can only give what we have now, and if we shall meet again in some far off place. It may be different for us, but I will always hold these few weeks we spent in my heart forever. If you do get deployed and I am still there I will find you and I will come to you."

With tears forming in my eyes, I asked, "You will? He said, "Yeah, I can do that, I'm a Sergeant Major." I said, "Yes, I believe you will." He kissed me and we made love right there on the floor in front of the fireplace. We then laid in each other's arms and dozed off asleep.

I awoke when I felt him move. It was beginning to get dark outside. He said, "I'm going to put a log on the fire it's a little chilly. I said, "Grab a blanket, and I'll get the wine and cheese." "I brought some strawberry too." "Great, we'll have a picnic right here on the floor in front of the fire."

The phone rang I grabbed the living room phone. It was Jackie. She called to let me know she was back in LA. She said, "She called to give me that information I needed for my deployment packet at DA." I said, "Thanks." She gave me a number and the point of contact. She said, "I'll give you a call before I deploy. It didn't take me long to get my orders. Your POC is a Master Sergeant Davies. We got really tight. Tell him I told you to call." I said, "Ok, thanks a lot Jackie."

Daniel put a log on the fire and we sat and watched it burn. He sat down next to me and said, "Honey, I know this is a conversation you don't want to talk about any more. What do you want to do on our last days here together?" "I don't know you make it sound so final." "It may be." "I don't want to think of that. I really don't know.

We've had so many wonderful times together, sunrises, sunsets walks along the beach or just sitting like now in front of the fireplace and nurturing each other's company. I'm going to leave that up to you." "Ok, well, I've got some plans to make." "I guess you have." He threw another log on the fire. "When you going to actually move into the new place?" "I guess tomorrow, I can't keep putting it off."

"Well, since you already have your keys, we can do that tomorrow, and they will deliver the furniture sometime tomorrow?" "Yeah, they said about ten o'clock they should be there. That way we can get everything set up and have the rest of the day to ourselves."

"Sounds great that way I can make love to my best girl, the first night in her new place." "I guess you're right." "When are you going to get your phone transferred?" I can do that tomorrow also all it takes is a phone call." "Well looks like you got a plan, and you have worked everything out."

I got up and walked to the sliding doors and said, "This may be our last night here in the Penthouse and here she comes." "What the fog?" "She's moving fast tonight, she must be in a hurry. I think she knows I'm here every night, looking for her. She knows, I won't be standing here, after tonight." "You speak of it as a person."

"I know. She's been here with me every night I can remember, since I moved into this apartment, looking up at me as I looked down at her. She has been my friend, I will miss her presence." Daniel took his usual place behind me and put his arms around my shoulders and said, "As I will miss your every presence," and kissed my neck. I kissed his arms around my shoulder.

I asked, "You ready to go to bed?" "Not yet, I've got to run down to my place for a minute." "I'm going to stand here for a while." "I won't be long." "I'll wait. "Ok," and kissed me on the top of my head and patted me on my butt. I stood and looked out at the double light moving together disappearing in the fog as it got dense.

I felt the burning in my nose as the tears began to roll down my cheeks. I went to the bathroom and got a tissue to wipe my eyes. I looked at myself in the mirror and said, "I've got to get through this, I can do this." I heard the door opened, I ran the shower. Daniel said, "Where you at?" "I was going to take a shower." "You alright?"

He walked in the bathroom and stood in front of my naked body and asked, "You haven't been crying?" "No." "You liar, your eyes are red." I laid my head on his chest as he said, "I know babe, I know. We just have to be strong and I need you to be strong for me. I can't do this if you fall apart on me, now." I wiped my eyes and said, "Ok."

I then got in the hot steamy shower. Daniel opened the sliding door and said, "Can I join you?" "Sure."

He climbed in and took the body wash and started to wash my back and lower back side. He then said, "We've never made love in the shower before." "I know." He turned me around and said, "Come here babe." He rinsed the soap off me and started kissing my breast and belly button. He then lifted me up and set me on top of him as he slide inside of me. We made love with him standing and holding me up in the shower as the overhead shower steaming up the whole bathroom.

He gently let me down and opened the shower door and said, "Come here." He led me to the bed and lifted me up and sat me back on top of him as he slide back inside of me. We sat on the bed facing each other with him inside of me. I thought I was going to faint. He laid back and massaged my body inside and out all over. He then sat up and lifted me up and turned me over on the bed without missing a beat. I said, "Damn this man got skills." We both had worked up a sweat and exhausted from such intense love making.

Daniel got up and cut the shower off and said, "It like a steam bath in here." "We can always sleep in the other bedroom." He said, "That's right," and picked me up and carried me into the other bedroom. He then said, "At least the blankets aren't wet." "But you are." "You too" and pulled me close to him, "You feel better now?"

"Yes, you've worked all that grief and sadness out of me." "Glad I could be of help." I laid on my stomach. He turned on his and put his long leg across my butt and his arm across my back and said, "Now, you can't get away from me." "Never!" He kissed my shoulder and said, "Good! Now get some sleep." We both drift off to sleep.

Daniel woke up first. I asked, "Why you getting up so early?" He said, "I heard the alarm off in the distance. I got to go by the battalion for a moment. I should be back shortly. I just got to drop some things off." "Ok, I should be up by then." He threw on his PT sweats and kissed me on my forehead.

He then said, "We should be able to move that stuff of yours this morning. We could use both cars." "That'll be great, that way we can make just one trip and be there when the furniture arrive. I was thinking about asking the Command Sergeant Major for one more day on my pass so we can have tomorrow to ourselves." "I was hoping you would do that. I may have a surprise for you." "Oh yeah, oh boy, is it a good or bad surprise?" "Oh, it's good." He gave me a gentle kiss on my butt and gave it a hard tap and said, "Now, get up, I should be back shortly."

I got up and got in the shower. I thought back over the previous day, I said to myself that was a very emotional day. If I get through tomorrow without falling apart I should be alright when he leaves on Sunday. Four more days, and Daniel will be gone. I felt my heart sunk. I said stop; stop thinking about it. You have been through worse. He did say if I get deployed he will find me. I got out the shower and threw on a set of Army sweats and hoodie.

I had started stacking things along the wall near the door. I had cleared out the boxes in the bedroom when I heard the door open. I heard Daniel say under his breath, "Damn babe, you must be really motivated." "I am, we should get most of this in the cars. Things I can't get in now we can get later today." He said, "That's great, hand me your keys, I'll start loading both cars."

In less than an hour we had both cars loaded. Daniel stuck out his hand and said, "Come here babe, I got something to show you. I said what?" It was a little tannish brown Chrysler convertible with a cream colored top. It was really cute. He said "I told you I had a surprise for you and I did say I was going to help you find a "Hoopdee" to get around in." "You didn't?"

"When I saw the picture in the PX the other day, for sale. I knew it was perfect for you." "I found it, but you have to pay for it. The soldier whom it belongs to, deployed on the first wave. He tried to sell it but his time ran out. He had to leave before he could sell it." I looked inside and started it up.

"I've driven it and you will get good gas mileage. He took good care of it. It's a four cylinder that's all you need around here in the city." "I love it. It's just what I needed. How much does he want for it?" "$2000.00, but I talked them down to $1500.00 cash." "I can do

My Forbidden Love

that. I can pay them today." I gave him a big kiss on the jaw just in case someone was in the parking garage looking.

He said, "Ok, let's get this show on the road. We'll go by your new place and get this stuff unloaded and wait for the furniture people. We can go take the money to that soldier's spouse." "That sound like a plan. Oh, Sergeant Major I'm so happy. I got a car. He looked at me and said, "Sergeant Major."

I put both hands out and turn my head. He said, "I get your drift." As we walked back to our cars, I said, "Don't forget where you are." He said, "You right keep me on point." "See that's why you have me around. You have to remember when you leave I will still be around here." "I know you got my back." "That's ok Sergeant Major, I got your back."

When we got to the cars, he said I wished we didn't have to play these games. He said, "Don't forget to call Command Sergeant Major you need an extension on that pass. I already mentioned it to him, just give him a call." I said "Ok, I'll call him after I call the phone company."

When we got to my new place the furniture people were there waiting for us. I let them in while Daniel unloaded both cars. They had everything set up in all rooms within an hour. We left everything in the middle of the floor and up against the walls. He asked, "When you going to turn your keys into the Penthouse?"

"Probably Saturday since you're leaving Sunday." He said, "That's right, if you want to, we can stay there one more night. Your lease isn't up until Saturday." "When are you turning yours' in?" "I'll drop mine off Saturday, also. That way I can help you get settled in here before I leave. So I get to make love to you one more time in the Penthouse." "I guess you will.

We went and got the money to pay for the car. We dropped the money off and got the bill of sale and the other papers on the vehicle. I followed Daniel to the airport to drop off the mustang at Dollar Rental. We then drove back to the new place to try and set things up.

I called the phone company to get the phone changed over but that would not happen until the next day. We went back to the

Penthouse and I called CSM for an extension on my pass. He said, "Not a problem. I'll see you on Thursday." I said, "Thank you CSM." When I got off the phone, Daniel asked, "You straight."

I put up my thumb and said, "I'm straight. So, what we going to do now? We had a pretty productive day." "I thought we get dress and go out to that place Tom took us the Clift House Restaurant. I made reservation for seven. I thought we might drive over to Sausalito first. I found a perfect spot we can watch the sunset and then go to dinner. Just put on something comfortable. I'll bring a blanket just in case your friend the fog shows up before we leave.

I put on a pair of slacks and white cow neck cable sweater. We left early before the rush hour traffic started to leave the city. We crossed the Golden Gate Bridge and made a left turn on a road that took you to the hills that over looked the Golden Gate Bridge and the city in the background. We parked at the lookout point overlooking the channel to the "Puget Sound". The traffic was just beginning to pick up on the bridge leaving the city.

Daniel got out the car and sat on the front of the hood. "Now you know where that lady called "Fog" comes from at night as she creeps into the city. As we look up the channel, we could see the fog rising from the cool water coming from the north as it comes down the channel.

The sun was just beginning to make its move to go to rest. As we looked straight across the bridge, the sun started to settle in the distance on the water. Its orange reflection shimmered on the surface of the water as it slipped slowly into the line that separated the sky and the water. It gave a bright glow as a last effort to show its strength and then suddenly slipped behind the water line. I told Daniel, "I can never get enough of the sunrises and sunsets. I believe it's God's way of showing us everything has a beginning and an ending, just as we do.

Whenever I see a sunset it will always give me fond memories we spent on the cove at Morro's Bay and this moment here at the top of the world away from all the traffic and the hustling and bustling of the city and the world around us, as the day slips away from our very sight.

This is a very beautiful place. You can look to your left and see darkness moving in over the city and the speckle of lights coming on in the city; and if you look to your right you can see my friend "fog" moving slowly towards the harbor to take her place until the sun rises in the morning and run her off. She will disappear until the next night she gets to show her face again."

"Val, you have an eye for expressing the beauty you see in things. You should become a writer." "I told you I'm going to write my memoirs and I will dedicate a whole chapter to you." "I would surely look for it when it comes out."

"I will autograph it." "It's getting late we need to get across the bridge if we want to make our reservation." "I hope we can sit outside. I want to feel the fog when she rolls in." "We'll see." I gave him a peck on the chin and grabbed his arm as he walked me to my side of the car.

CHAPTER

Eight

The traffic was heavy. We arrived ten minutes before our reservations. Daniel asked for an outside table. The maître d' said, "It's going to be chilly outside but we have the center fireplace on." He showed us to our table and said, "Enjoy your meal; your waiter will be right with you." We looked at the menu and decided what we were going to eat. I chose shrimps as usual. Daniel chose oysters. I said, "As if you needed them."

He smiled and said, "Oh look, we have company. It was Command Sergeant Major Douglas and his wife Diane. I stood when he came to the table." "You don't have to do that, Val. Some habits are hard to break. He said, "How are things going with the move" as he held his wife's chair to sit.

I said "I'm almost there. I just have a few things that need closure." "I'm sure you do." Daniel said, "We haven't ordered yet." CSM asked, "So what's good (a kind way of asking what you getting?")

Daniel said, "I'm going to try the steam Oysters and she's getting the breaded Shrimp (that's because I didn't know any better)." CSM said, "Oysters, man you sure you want to try those?" Daniel said, "Yeah man, why not?" They both laughed CSM said, "If you're game, I guess I'll try them too, have she decided?" "I'm going to try the scallops." "What are you drinking?" "Let's get some Chablis white, if that's ok. "Yeah, that's good."

When the waiter came Command Sergeant Major did the order for the table. I asked, is that protocol?" Command Sergeant Major said, "It doesn't matter, we're civilians tonight. That's right you used to work at the Pentagon for the Chief of Staff of the Army, General Wickham and the current TRADOC Commander Lt General Thurman." I said, "Yes, I did CSM, but he was the Vice Chief of Staff at that time." He gave me that look again.

Man, you do have some mileages on your resume'." I said, "That was a civil service position." He said, "That doesn't matter. How long you work for them?" "About four years until I moved to LA." "You'll be here for a while, your mobilization orders are for a year." "Yeah, I know." "You know you could get deployed if that fool doesn't heed to our warning!

Daniel was shaking his head in agreement. I said, "Oh well, I don't have a problem with that." Command Sergeant Major said, "I know you don't," and looked at Daniel. (*I said to myself all shit*).

The waiter brought us a Carafe of Chablis. Daniel poured the wine. Command Sergeant Major, lifted his glass and said toast, "To a very good friend who I will truly miss when he's gone, he looked directly in his eyes and said, don't try to be a hero" Daniel said, "Yes Command Sergeant Major.

We all raise our glasses and tap. Daniel then said, "Toast to friends who I know I will truly miss. Thank you for your friendship (to Command Sergeant Major), your hospitality (to Diane) and your love (to me)." I looked at him and bucked my eyes. Command Sergeant Major said, "Oh we know give us a break." We tapped glasses and sipped our wine. I couldn't say anything. I just sat there and thought to myself *"awkward moment"*.

Diane broke the moment by saying excuse me, "Val, would you walk with me to the ladies room?" "Sure." I couldn't get up quick enough. As we walked to the ladies room, Diane said, "Val, you have to excuse Tom. He can be a bit direct sometimes."

I said, "Excuse me Diane, for my abruptness, but he is, a Command Sergeant Major, and in my world, he can get as direct as he want, and don't have to apologize for it." I thought to myself, she must really think I'm one of his weak minded soldiers.

Trying to explain herself, Diane said, "I know that, but he knows exactly how the both of you feel about each other. Tom and Dan have been friends a long time. They went to Sergeant Major's academy together and a lot of history is with those two, but they are very good friends.

He likes you a lot, as a soldier, and thinks and speaks highly of you. He thinks of Dan as a brother, as well as a brother in arms. He knows about Dan's relationship with his wife, but as a friend he can't and won't get involved." "I don't need to know all this." In a somewhat spiteful manner, she pressed on "Oh, but you do. Dan has fallen head over heels in love with you, and he doesn't know what to do. He's got to make this deployment, if he wants to make Command Sergeant Major like his friend." "I understand. I wouldn't do anything to destroy his chance of promotion.

You sound like there's some doubt, in him making this deployment. He's looking forward to this deployment. I cannot imagine Daniel getting this far in his career, and then let some three week fling destroy it. He knows this could be his career advancement, or it could be a career ender. He's come too far to let this happen. I'll talk to him about it."

She finally said, "Ok, I know you'll do the right thing. You know, how the system works." "I'll fix this tonight, Ok." She said, "Ok."

We walked back to the table. Our food had arrived. CSM asked, "Everything alright? I thought I had to come in there and get you ladies." (I know, he didn't think he hurt my feelings) He looked at Diane and asked, "Are we straight?" She looked at me and said, "We're good." Daniel said "Let's eat. There's nothing worse than cold seafood."

CSM asked me where I was from (just to break the ice). I told him, "From a place called Charlottesville, VA." "I know where that is. It's where the Army JAG School is, about 100 miles from DC." "That is correct, it's a small college town where the University of VA." "Orange and blue, the Virginia Cavaliers."

Diane broke the two way conversation and asked Daniel, are you all packed?" He said, "I been packed since I got my warning order." CSM asked, "You finish out processing?" "Yeah, all I got left to do is sign out of the battalion tomorrow." CSM said, "Don't try to slip out; the Colonel's having an award ceremony for you tomorrow." He asked me, "You gonna be there tomorrow?"

I said, "I don't think so. I have to finish clearing my apartment at the Towers." CSM asked, "So when does your group go to the MOB site?" "We're going Friday. Our orders dated 1 December. So we have to out process and in process as mobilization soldiers."

He said, "That sound a bit confusing, but I guess you know what you are doing." "It's just a little management of the budgets. We have to be out the system in order for DA to put us in the system. So in order to be mobilized, we have to come off our current orders. Then have a one day break; and then process into our MOB Site as Mobilized soldier.

According to DA you cannot have a soldier having overlapping orders. So in order to fix that you would have to bring the reserve soldier off order and give them a one day break so they won't have continuing orders which puts the person on order for more than maximum number of days; and then they are no longer considered title 10 reservist on active duty. They are then considered a regular soldier on full time active duty and they can receive the same benefits as a Regular Army soldier.

So, that is why the EOC, will have to be closed for one day or we would need to get our orders amended. CSM said, "I didn't know that. How did you know that?" "CSM, I've been on more short tours than you can count on both hands at the Support Command; and every time I came off orders, I had a new set of orders. Each time I had to take a one day break because of title 10 guidelines."

He then said, "See if you can come by the office tomorrow so we can work this out. Your people may have to take that one day break on Thursday or Friday and then MOB on Sunday or Monday."

Daniel said, "That was confusing, yet interesting. Why's that so?" "It's all about budget constraints. We all know it's easy to put reservist on active duty because they are a part of the federal force. It was a way to put reserve soldiers on active duty without giving them full benefit.

It's a way of keeping the drilling reservist and National Guard soldiers separate from the Regular Army budget. A little something Congress' "Armed Services Committee" did to fix the shortage of troops and boots on the ground."

CSM said, "SSG Acoma you seem to be very knowledgeable about these matters." "It's just a matter of keeping your eyes and ears open, at all times when assigned in the command group. That way you already know the answers and one doesn't need to ask questions."

Daniel looked around and said, "It's getting late and it's about time we call it a night." CSM said, "Looks like they're waiting for us to turn out the lights. So, we got up and started towards the door. Daniel started to pick up the check and said, "You're my guest." CSM said, "You're the one, that's going to the desert. It's my treat, you get the next one."

Daniel said, "I'll hold you to that." We waited as CSM paid the tab. Daniel said, "At least let me leave the tip." CSM said, "I took care of that already."

As we walked to the few cars left in the parking lot, CSM said, Val, I know you are still trying to put some closure on your personal business, but I appreciate if you stop by my office tomorrow about 13:00; that should give you some time to take care of anything that you have to do in the morning.

We need to see, what I need to do about our earlier discussion; that way I can pick your brain some more. We split and went to our cars. CSM then said, "Dan don't forget the awards ceremony at 10:00." He said, "Hoooah, Command Sergeant Major see you then." We got in our cars and drove off.

"That was an interesting evening of event." "I'm serious, for a minute there, I felt like I was the villain." "What did Diane say to you that made y'all take so long in the rest room?" "First, it wasn't all Diane, I had a few things to say also and it wasn't about blaming either of us. It was mostly about you making the correct and sound decision.

They actually think you are so in love with me, you are willing to jeopardize your career, and the opportunity for advancement to Command Sergeant Major. They are bigger fools than I thought they were.

I told her you are not that stupid or so weak minded to do something like that. I didn't put it in those words, but she got the message. I told her you would not give up something you been working towards your whole life, and career. Not just for a three week fling." He interrupted and asked, "Wait a minute. Is that what you call this?"

"No, no honey not at all, but that's what they think it is. I had to convince her that it's not at all, what they think it is." "Oh, I was getting a little misunderstanding there, I'm sorry." "Love means, never having to say you're sorry." He took my hand and kissed the back of it. "Where we going the old or the new?"

"Daniel, you aren't having doubt about your deployment?" "No not at all. I want this. I need this. I trained very hard and trained other soldiers hard just for this." "I was a little concerned. You have been somewhat evasive the past few days." "I was just trying to put closure on some personal things, so we can have these last few days to ourselves. You still didn't answer my question. "You make the decision. He turned in the direction of the penthouse and said, decision made." (I thought to myself Just like a Sergeant Major).

Daniel opened the door since he still had his key. I said, "She looks so lonesome." He walked over and cut the stereo on and said, "Not for long." Lionel Richie's greatest hits began to play. I sat on the sofa and lean my head against the back of the sofa. He asked, "You tired? We still have a little wine left." "I'll take just a little." He took the glasses that came with the apartment and poured two half glasses. He handed me mine. I sipped a little and sat it on the end table.

He stood between me and the fireplace and sat his glass on the mantle. He pulled me up in his arms and said, "You know we've never danced together." "Would you dance with me My Lady?" "Yes." He held me close and sang the words along with Lionel as he sang "Three Times a Lady" we danced our first and last dance together.

I laid my head against his chest and began to cry as I heard the words "Come to the end of our Rainbow". He lifted my chin and looked in my eyes with his eyes beginning to tear and with a smile, shook his head and said, "No tears babe, no tears." I smiled and shook my head up and down and whispered, "Ok." He stopped dancing and still holding my hand, he walked me to our favorite spot at the balcony window looking out at the fog.

"Let's not make this a sad occasion with my leaving. We have so many beautiful memories right here in this apartment. Let's not spoil it with tears and talking about what people said. In a couple of days this'll all be behind us; and all we'll have are the memories.

Val, my love, I want to thank you for the memories those beautiful memories. I know we will meet again. I feel it in my heart." He turned me facing him and said, "This is not the end I will find you wherever you may be, because I love you so very much.

You are smart and sharp; and don't let anyone tell you anything different. I envy your husband; who doesn't know how fortunate he is to have such a jewel in his crown. You are a diamond and I wish you were mine's forever."

"You are such a romantic, and poetic. How can I let you go, but I know it is something, I have got to do." He slowly pulled my sweater over my head and kissed my breast. He then said, "They're very beautiful" and then kissed my neck. "Do you remember the first time we made love?"

I said, "No." "Yes you do; you a bad liar." I said, "Ok, yes I do every moment and every movement. I remember we were almost standing in this very same place. We had just a little too much Mateus; and you walked me to my bedroom, as you are doing now. You laid me on the bed and slowly undressed me. You kissed my neck, breast, and belly button. I think that was all." He said, "What, you forgot." "No my memory went blank." "Well let me give you a little refresher." He slid my slacks down to my knees and kissed me below my belly button and then kissed me lower.

He then came and lied beside me. I said, "You didn't do that." "I drew a blank, so I ad lib." "In that case." I kicked off my pants and started to undress him beginning with his pants first and then his shirt. I kissed his tight chest and then his belly button. He said, "Ok lady, it's my turn."

He stood up and pulled me to the end of the bed and placed my legs over his shoulders and slowly slid inside of me. I reached for him and he sat me up with my legs still over his shoulders. He didn't say anything but formed his lips as to kiss me and then winked as to say "I got you". I couldn't do anything but to fall back in surrender. He really got me that round. But I gave him a go for his money. We both fell out from exhaustion.

CHAPTER Nine

I was still asleep when Daniel woke me and said, "I'll see you later." He gave me a peck on the forehead and left. I told him "Ok." I turned over and slept until the alarm went off at eleven o'clock. I got up and showered and put my BDUs on. I always kept in the car.

I got to the Command Sergeant Major office about 12:45 for our 13:00 meeting. He was standing in his office door. He said "Come on in Sergeant Acoma." "Hoooah, Command Sergeant Major." I asked, "How was the awards ceremony?" "It was really nice. Sergeant Major Howard got a "Meritorious Service Medal". All the other deploying soldiers got "Army Commendation Medal" and "Army Achievement Medal". You know they don't give Sergeant Major those awards." "I know."

He then changed the subject and said, "We had to do some changes and research because of the information you laid on me last night. I found out that everything you said is true and correct; you and all your soldiers on short tours have to take a day off before reporting to Camp Parks as your MOB Site.

That means those soldiers in the EOC will come off orders today. This is their last working day on short tour. You will take tomorrow as your break in service day. On Saturday you will report to Camp Parks at 07:30 for in processing. Upon completion of your in processing you will report back here to the EOC for sign-in.

Your next duty day will begin at 07:30 except days we have PT. You will be the NCOIC for the MOB Site processing. Your team's work schedule will be the same as it was when you were on tour. Do you have any questions Staff Sergeant Acoma?" I said, "No, Command Sergeant Major." "You will need transportation to get to Parks. Do you have a soldier that has a military driver's license?" "Yes, Command Sergeant Major, Sergeant Bigalowe does." "Good have Bigalowe sign out a 16 Pax from the Motor Pool by COB today and tell him to park it in the military vehicle parking space so he can drive the MOB Site people on Saturday.

I expect a departure time NLT 05:30. I need you to now go talk to your people and explain to them what you told me last night. When you get through I need you to report back here to me." I said, "Yes Command Sergeant Major."

I went down to the EOC and told the soldiers everything I was told with the EOC OIC supporting my information. I then returned back to Command Sergeant Major Douglas' office. It was about 16:00. Everyone had gone for the day. Command Sergeant Major said, "Come on in Sergeant.

First, I wanted you to hear this from me. Sergeant Major Howard has left for deployment. I took him to the airport about 11:00 right after the award ceremony. He had a 14:00 flight. I had a long discussion with him; and I suggested that although he is no longer a member of this command, it is my responsibility as a Command Sergeant Major and his friend to look out for his best interest. I told him I thought he had gotten too involved with you, Staff Sergeant Acoma and I did not want to see him screw up his career.

I also feel the same about you. I have a lot of respect for you as a soldier and I see you also as a friend. We have formed a little bit of history and a friendship that I deeply respect. I found you to be one of the most knowledgeable NCOs at your rank, as a Staff Sergeant, I've come across in a very long time.

Sergeant Acoma, Val I stood by and watch you two falling deeply in love with each other. I have no doubt about it. But although the Army is the largest branch of service, it is also a small community of people. Although you might not know it, or want to know it, people see you or they saw you.

I have to admit you two did very well keeping it under wraps' but that's not cutting the cake. You are a Staff Sergeant and Dan is a Sergeant Major. You both knew better but you let your feelings take you to a level where someone had to step in and try to fix the situation. I could not take the chance of Dan intentionally missing movement. That is a Court Martial Offense, if it is not an emergency.

I just could not take a chance without doing something about it. So I convinced Dan to catch the next flight out of here. He has come a long way to make Sergeant Major. He is the best ordnance soldier I ever known. If it wasn't for Dan I probably would not have made it through Sergeant Major academy. So now it was time I paid him back.

So I just want you to know I am happy for my friend. He's finally found that true love. But the timing is wrong for both of you. I was just afraid you both would have been brought up on fraternization charges. I could not take a chance on that. So Val that is why I did what I had to do, for you who will still be here; and Dan who needed to move on and for the good of the Army and my sanity.

So, are you going to be alright? I see you are a little upset. I can understand, but I was hoping you understand, why I did what I had to do.

I finally had the strength to say something. I told myself I was not going to make it long. "Command Sergeant Major I truly understand what you did, and why you did it, with no animosity.

We knew it was getting out of hand and I'm sure you and him had a lot of conversation reference our relationship. But there was never any doubt whether Sergeant Howard was going to leave when his time came. We were only trying to relish the time until he had to leave. I admit things did get a lot out of hand but we had each other career and marriages in mind.

Daniel was going to leave. This was going to be our last night together. But maybe it's best to leave it at that. We both can get on with our lives and careers. I'm alright and I understand you did this for both Sergeant Major Howard and me." "You sure you going to be alright?"

"I'm sure, Command Sergeant Major." "I can give you a lift to which ever place you're staying. You have a few days before coming back on duty. Get some rest and try to clear your thoughts. I got up and said thanks Command Sergeant Major and left his office.

It was getting dark. I was not ready for my new apartment. This day had been a total disaster as far as I was concerned. Since I was off tomorrow I decided to go buy me a bottle of Mateus and sit in the penthouse and watch the fog come in. I would spend all day tomorrow working on my deployment packet.

CHAPTER

Ten

I opened the door and thought to myself, I can still smell his scent. I went in the kitchen and looked in the dishwasher for a glass. I said, "I know I washed those glasses." I heard a voice say "Hey Babe you miss me", I looked at him and my eye bucked almost out of my head. "Oh, **SHIT**.

I thought you were gone." "I am, in a way. I'm not in the unit and I'm not on a plane to Fort Lewis, WA. either" "Then what are you doing here? CSM find out you didn't get on that plane; he'll have both our asses."

"Tell me about it. Well, I got in line to check my bags in and I thought about how I was leaving and not giving you a word that I was gone. So, I stayed in line and change my reservation until tomorrow the same time. I rented a car and threw my bags in the trunk, and here I am. Babe, I couldn't just all of a sudden leave and not let you know why and how."

"Command Sergeant Major said enough to make the point. I just left his office maybe an hour ago. That whole scene was just unreal. I'm off tomorrow I could go to the airport with you and catch the shuttle back." "On second thought you don't want to be seen at the airport, less more with me." "Yeah, you right."

"I just want to be with you, hold you and maybe not even make love, but spend these last few hours being with you." "Are you hungry?"

My Forbidden Love

"No not really." "We could order an after sex food." He chuckled a little "Oh you mean a pizza." "Yeah; you order, have it delivered."

"So what were you going to do; if I were gone?" "Open a bottle of Mateus and get high. Talk to the fog, and go to bed early. I thought you leaving would be a smooth transition, but it got out of hand."

"That was not my intention. I let my friend convince me I was in a relationship that I had no control of." "I still want to believe he had your best interest at heart, my question to you is how would you had handled this situation if you were CSM?"

"I think I would have handled it the same way. It seems he put a lot of thought in this. Him and Diane I believe." I said, "Yeah, to go so far as to have you hurry up and sign out of the unit; and take you to the airport."

"Honey, let me tell you how this all went down. I told you I went running with Tom a few days ago. I taped the whole conversation. Tom's my friend but he's career oriented too." "I know, I noticed that today."

"When I told him, I was in love with you. He hit the roof. He said, man haven't you learned anything from me? I cursed him out. I told him, man she knows this. He said damn that's even worse, now I got two of you. What's going to happen when you leave?

I'm going to have an Irate, frantic female NCO who's going to need to go to mental health, because she had fallen in love with a god-damn Sergeant Major. Not just any Sergeant-Major but my god-damn Sergeant-Major. He said now Sergeant Major what the "Fuck" you think I suppose to do. Let it fade away.

He said that's a god-damn lie. Women don't let that kind of Shit, just fade away. They are like an alligator in a swamp. They hold on to shit, to the very end. They don't give a fuck, their feelings been hurt, that comes first.

You should know better. You got a wife who don't want you but don't want to divorce you either, because she don't want you to have anyone either. He said talk about a set of vice-grips. Your nuts must be really hurting. Daniel said man she's not like that. We have a very good understanding, from the very beginning.

He said yeah man that's what they all say. I'm not saying she is or will be a basket case. I'm just saying I don't want to have to clean up no shit, after you are gone.

Dan said man I tell you what, I'm going to take Val to dinner tomorrow. Some place nice as our farewell dinner together. Why don't you and Diane meet us there and you will see for yourself. What's that place we went to after the Opera? Command Sergeant Major said ooh the Opera that's the whole cause of all this shit.

Dan said what's the name of the restaurant man? Tom said the "Clift House Restaurant". He said I'll make the reservation and let you know what time. Dan said don't make them too late or too early we have another engagement.

I said, "Is that it. It seems to me it doesn't matter what was said or done at the restaurant. He already had his mind made up. CSM just didn't want his career on the line. He did what he thought was best for the current situation. Get rid of the "biggest threat". You my darling were the "biggest threat".

"You are so right. When senior officer or NCO get into situation or trouble, the Army always teaches you to get rid of the "biggest threat" that's "Combat 101". The threat that causes the most damage, get rid of it first. I was the biggest threat in his eyes and his career. So with me hurried out the picture, Command Sergeant Major can have a "plausible deniability". He could then deny ever having knowledge of any such situation. But in reality we both know that Sergeant Majors know everything going on in their units."

"He knew I was never a threat to his career, so also after last night, he realized I'm no threat to him. I know he had Diane, to put her two cents in it too. That trip to the rest room was staged just to get me and her alone.

She thought that I was just a lowly Staff Sergeant, but I am no one's dummy. She took me for a weak minded individual, but I broke it down to her. I made her believe that I saw our relationship as a mere fling. I'm sorry honey, I read that woman the day I set foot in their house on Thanksgiving Day.

You see honey in my previous civil service job and military career I have worked for seven generals all were Two stars or above and only one was never married General Maxwell Thurman, but he had two dogs.

But getting to the point, high ranking executive officers and NCOs who are married, their spouses think they wear the rank also. Some people fall for that mess, but I don't.

An old war horse by the name of Willie Lorbach, she was a chain smoking, beer drinking retired Sergeant First Class, in the Women's Army Corp, who worked in the office across the hall from General Thurman's, told me if any of those wives get out of hand tell them "I wear my rank on my sleeve, Where's yours".

Diane Douglas is one of those women. She thinks that since she is a Command Sergeant Major's wife, she has the same power as he does. What makes it so bad, he put that mess in her head, and she believes it. Your wife probably feels the same way.

But they are not the one, who went through what you went through, to get that Rank. Oh, they might have sat at home and mind the house and kids, but they didn't earn that rank. So they think, they can stand, and tell me about what it takes for you, to get on that plane, and go fight a war. Hell No!

But I, damn sure can, because I know, one day my turn will come also. She was trying to punk me, because she was scared, her husband was going to get caught up in something that he knew was going on.

So honey, I gave her what she needed to take back to her husband. I'm pretty sure she told him, I was no threat to him, once he got rid of you. Daniel asked, "Why you say that?"

"Honey, look at it this way, if you really think about it. If two soldiers involved, let's say one is a "Sergeant" and the other is a "Staff Sergeant" like me and they are both married to someone else. The Commander gives both an Article 15 and orders them to cease any means of communication ever again.

Now take us for instance. What will happen to us? You Sergeant Major Howard would be forced into early retirement. Command Sergeant Major Douglas would be forced into early retirement also.

Me as a Staff Sergeant they could do a couple of things to me, Court Martial, Article 15 or whatever the Commander sees fit. But the thing behind this is, the Army does not look at age and say "You are old enough to know better" the Army looks at rank.

They would say since I am a lower rank, than the senior Non-commissioned Officers (NCO) involved. I would not be the most, remind you I said the most responsible, individual involved.

The most responsible person or persons involved are you, Sergeant Major Howard and Command Sergeant Major Douglas because he was aware of the situation plus he was the one who introduced and suggested we have our first encounter.

You see honey I didn't just work in the Pentagon. I worked for the Vice Chief of Staff of the Army, a Four Star General who wore taps on, the heels and toes of his shoes and boots; so when people heard him coming they would step aside or clear the hallway. He told me one day it's not what you know Val it's who you know. He told me that, just before I transferred to the unit in Los Angeles.

I became the executive secretary to the Commanding General of a two star command, and later the Center's Executive Administrator Assistant. I got the job, as the General's secretary not only because of what I knew, but also because of who I knew; and that man now runs TRADOC.

He called me and congratulated me on getting the job. If he saw the mess I have gotten in, he would be a bit surprised, but not disappointed. Another one of Thurman famous Quotes "People can surprise me; but only I can disappoint myself."

"So you think Command Sergeant Major believed, that I may be a threat to his career if I stayed here until I deployed. So, that's why he worked so hard to get me out of here." "Honey that's because he was always looking out for "Numero Uno", and if by some strange coincident he helped you in this process, then you are also home free. But you had to come back." I pinched him. He said, "Ouch! That wasn't nice."

"I almost hit the roof myself when you told me, you told Command Sergeant Major that you were in love with me." "I just wanted my closest friend to know, I had found me someone who I love and love me too. Tom was always telling me, man you need to find you, a good woman. He even mentioned you, one day you came in the NCO club to get lunch. I asked was she married. He said I don't know, I didn't notice a ring.

You see I had been eyeing you, since the day you came up from Roberts with those packets from those AT units. I said, "I didn't see you. I know, I would have noticed you." He said, "I'm sure you know now, I was the one who got all the National Guard unit's packets after you gave them to Command Sergeant Major Douglas."

"At that time I never knew where they went after I gave them to him." "I reviewed them and forwarded them after I coded them deployable or non-deployable to their State headquarters and to National Guard headquarters at the Pentagon, your old stomping ground." I smiled.

"You would be amazed how in our world, with the Army, it's nothing but a big circle that keeps revolving around itself. It all leads back here to us in the EOC on one piece of paper telling a unit, they are deploying to fight a war."

"You right babe, in a way it started right here in our two hands. He grabbed me and said come here babe, I haven't held you since you walked in that door."

"It has been a very interesting day, what if Command Sergeant Major found out you didn't get on that plane." "He can't touch me now. I'm not a part of his unit as of today. I am currently in transit and I have until 07:00 Monday morning to report to my MOB Site." "In that case I'm all yours."

The pizza had arrived during our probing the situation. He took off his BDU jacket and hung it around the back of the dining room chair. He handed me a plate for my pizza. He asked, "What you going to do now?" "I'm working on my next move maybe, deployment. I'm already mobilized."

"You don't want that. You don't know what you getting yourself in." "Oh, but I do. I might not be combat trained, but I am a soldier, and I have a role to play in this war. You know the slogan "Be all you can be in the United States Army" that's me.

I got out once and almost lost my dream. But by some strange coincident I got my dream back. I still haven't reached my goal in the Army and I have a long way to go. Who knows someday I might be a Sergeant Major or a First Sergeant. That's my real goal.

When I was at the Corps Support Command the Commanding General put me on fast track. I been to all my NCO schools even ANCO. I'm only waiting to submit my packet for promotion to E7. The unit has that all ready for submission to the next senior board." "Damn that what I call a woman with a plan." "Now I'm working that plan."

"So, honey you are more than a three week fling to me. You are the man or should I say Sergeant Major, I fell in love with. These last three weeks has been better than any mental health doctor could ever do for me. We've had good discussion, good conversation, I have been able to renew my mind on what I want in life; and how I got where I am today. It's been a mental cleansing. But above it all I learn how love really should be, along with the excellent love making that goes along with it.

So, if we never see each other again, I truly believe in my heart we were destined to meet. I hoped I have been a help to you as you have been to me. Sometimes we need a little turmoil in our life to find our true self."

I got up holding my wine flute with both hands and walked towards the window to my favorite spot, for maybe the very last time. Daniel followed with his glass and the bottle of Mateus.

I stood and stared at the fog coming in slowly. We both still in our BDU trousers, boots and tee shirt. He came over and stood in his place behind and kissed me on my neck. I said, "I now know what it feels like to be romanced." "And, I know what it feels like to romance a real lady."

I asked, "What does it feel like?" He said, "It was beautiful." "It could only happen in the movies, like watching a "Tahitian Sunrise"." "Having brunch on a Sunday morning, at a quite seaside village, and lunch at the "Fisherman's Wharf"." "Taking a boat ride to Alcatraz and under the Golden Gate Bridge and along the Marina coastline.

That beautiful romantic candlelight dinner, along the bay. Our first and only movie date. The many romantic nights here in front of the fireplace listening to "Kenny G", Lionel Richie and Frankie Beverly and Maze drinking Mateus and eating cheese and strawberries."

"The first time we made love, and when you gave me that very enticing massage and you to me also." Daniel then said, "The first time we made love in the shower, a wet and wild situation." "You are quite strong." "I lift weights that weigh more than you." "So that's your secret?" "I'll never tell."

"Speaking of secret, why do you always stand behind me when I'm standing here?" "I just like feeling your nice firm behind rub against my private." "So it's all about foreplay and you getting aroused." "Yeah, something like that, but how can I resist rubbing against all that." He gave my behind a push with his private. I felt his firmness grow in his trousers." "Ooh, you're right," I then said not tonight babe this is talk night. It's all about closure." "Ok, that's cool, but we'll see." I turned and kissed the tee shirt on his chest.

"So this is all about closure?" "Yeah, don't you think we should have closure? Since everyone wanted to put an end to it, for us. I just want to say one last thing and the conversation is over.

You knew I had to see the Command Sergeant Major this afternoon and why I didn't come to your award ceremony; Oh by the way congrats on the MSM. So, how the hell, he convinced you to leave after you signed out the unit? I've been trying to figure that out."

"Tom said, he was afraid you were not going to handle my departure very well. He said man she didn't want to show up, for your awards ceremony. She could have done that just to show support. I agreed with him.

"By the way, why didn't you show up?" "I wanted to, but I couldn't because after the awards, that's a sign of finality. I know I would have cried and people read through my tears."

"Babe, excuse me but that sounds like a piss poor excuse, for the NCOIC of the EOC. There were a lot of people crying. They were crying because soldiers were deploying not because of some other lame reason as that." "Alright already, I'm sorry I missed the ceremony."

"You ever thought that's one of the reasons that convinced me to leave. After all, we meant to each other. I wanted to see your face in formation more than anything else. I have to admit I was a little disappointed." "Remember what I said about disappointment. You can only disappoint yourself." "I was a little disappointed, but not in you."

"So that was the nail in the coffin that made you make the decision to leave." "In a way, but after the ceremony CSM made it seem so obvious. I was just hurt.

But then after I got to the airport I thought about it, maybe she couldn't stand the sight of me leaving. I just couldn't leave with you feeling this way and me either for that matter. These past three weeks had meant so much to the both of us. That's why I changed my reservation to the next flight out tomorrow. He looked at his watch and said or should I say later today.

When CSM dropped me off, he said he would explain everything to you. I said man let her down easy. She's a good person and a real lady. I don't want to hurt her. He said I got you man, I'll take care of it. We did our little hand shake and shoulder bump. He said man be careful and don't try to be no hero. I said Oh man I got this. He said ok man I got to go I told her to be there at 13:00. So that was it."

I said, "Command Sergeant Major Douglas why that conniving manipulating SOB. He made it seem that he felt we had gotten too involved with each other and we were being careless. He felt we were so madly in love he had to do something before we ruin both our careers. He also said he was looking out for your best interest as well as mine."

I took a big sip of the wine I had left in my glass. I continued, "After I got over the initial shock that you were gone. I listened to him and I said my peace.

I handled it very professionally and maintain my military bearing to the fullest. I told him I understand what he did and he had our best interest at heart. I bear no animosity; but at no time did Daniel, Sergeant Major Howard have a notion to not deploy. We were going to spend our last night together. You were going to leave and we would have continued to get on with our regular lives.

I admitted things did get a lot out of hand, but we had each other's career and marriage in mind. I thanked him and I left. I really wanted to tell Command Sergeant Major that, now there may never be a closure. So I came here hoping to make my own closure but you beat me to it.

I was very shocked and surprised to see you; but I was really happy also. I really thought you were going without telling me good-bye or see you in the desert or some sort. I was so hurt also. So you see honey we hurt each other in a way and that is why I told you tonight will be all about closure.

We must find a way in this relationship to place everything in perspective. Go on with our lives before we found each other and learn from what we had here. I don't know about you but if I never fall in love again, I can at least say "I found real love, and love found me"." "So well put, my dear. I'm a little tired can we go to bed now." "Yeah, its 2:00 a.m. it's a good thing I'm off orders today. He mumbled and said oh yeah, that's right, you out the Army for what, one day. Ok and dozed off to sleep."

We slept until about ten. Daniel asked, "Why didn't you take my clothes off?" "Why didn't you take mine off?" "Good question I should have." I took my uniform off and laid them on the chair in the living room. Daniel said, "I need to get out here by noon." "Good time."

He then walked over to my naked body and put his hand on my breast and kissed them both and said I'm going to miss you guys. He then went into the living room and cut the stereo on and played Lionel Richie's song "Three times a Lady". He came up to me and moving to the music and sang the words "Thanks for the time you've given me. The memories are all in my mind. We have really come to the end of our rainbow babe."

"Yeah, but I'm not going to cry this time. He whispered and said, "Don't, you might make me cry." He then kissed my neck, my ear, my forehead, and then my other ear. He said, "Babe for old time sake. He stooped down and kissed my belly button and then below my belly.

He then picked me up by both legs and laid me on my back on the bed. He said, "Come here juicy, daddy's got something for you. He pulled my butt up on his long thighs and slowly slid inside me and bend over and climb on top of me as if he was doing pushups and said, "I just want to take it easy and relish these last moments together, just me inside you and feeling just what I will be missing in that desert."

He whispered very softly, "Don't move just let me do the work. I just need you to follow my lead." I whispered "Yes, Sergeant Major, yes." He nibbled my ear lobe and said, "You're so bad." I laid back and let him have his moment and it was all worth it. His movement was so smooth and soothing. I then melted like butter. And it was all over for me but the show.

He then turned over and laid beside me and said, "I will truly miss you my "Forbidden Love"." I said, "Forbidden" huh. He got up and kissed my belly and looked at the clock. Come take a shower with me. I need to be out of here by noon its 11:30 now.

I laid with my face in the spot he just got up and said to myself what I'm going to do when he's gone. He fulfilled my days. I then got up and got in the shower with him. He asked me, "How's the car running?" "It runs well." He asked for the body wash and washed me all over and said, "For old time sake."

I then washed him all over and said, "For old time sake." He rinsed off and climbed out the shower. "Come on we're burning daylight." I got out and threw on a pair of army sweats I brought up from the car the night before. He was in BDUs and said, "Ok babe this is it, you going to walk me to the car?" My heart dropped and said, "Yeah." We walked to the parking garage where he parked his car in his old parking space. Our cars were the only ones on that level.

He put his stuff in the car and said, "Well, babe this is it. He was holding both my hands and put them around his neck and pulled me closer to him. "Don't make this hard. Don't cry and don't look as I drive away. So kiss me hard and deep as if I was inside of you and remember don't look as I drive away. Softly I said, "Ok."

My Forbidden Love

He kissed me hard and deep with his tongue. He then patted me on my behind and said, as he walked away for old time sake. I said "Hoooah". He back up. Tooted and sped off. I had to look back with tears beginning to form in my eyes. I then ran to the elevator. I went to the apartment and looked out the balcony in our spot and said "good-bye my love".

The Gulf War
Desert Shield/Desert Storm

CHAPTER

Eleven

I sat on the sofa in front of the fireplace and thought to myself so many memories, for just a short period of time. I will sleep in my new apartment tonight. I decided to stick around the penthouse until about 2:30 in case there was a phone call.

At about 1:30 the phone rang. I heard the familiar deep voice say, "I told you don't look back" "I'm sorry I just couldn't help it. I had to get that last look." "I know I looked through my rearview. When you going to the new place?" "In about an hour." "I called to hear your voice just one more time, and tell you I left your key on the kitchen counter with a note." "Ok" and went to look for it.

"I got it." "Don't open the note until tonight." "Ok". He said "Right, just like I told you not to look back." "Are you really going to get on that flight this time?" "Yeah, I'm at the gate now. I just wanted to give you a call before I left, if I don't hear or see you.

I'll see you in the Desert." "Ok, and don't try to be no hero." "Why do people, always say that, ok? I love you. Got to go! Many kisses!" "Back at you my love." We hung up. I looked at the note where it said to" "My Forbidden Love". "Well the final Chapter of "My Forbidden Love".

I couldn't leave and go to the new place yet. I wasn't quite ready to let the memories go so suddenly. I stood in the sliding door window for the last time and watched the fog move in at a very slow pace. I said she's moving like I feel. I was having a hard time letting go.

I couldn't figure out whether it was the Penthouse or the memories that we made here in the Penthouse. I took a shower and thought about just a few hours ago Daniel was washing my body in this very spot and I washed his.

I got out the shower and dried myself and thought about the first time he gave me a massage after I got out of the shower. I laid back on my bed and thought about every place he touched me. I picked up the note he left me.

I opened the note with the words "My Forbidden Love" on it.

"My Love, This is not our final good-bye. Thank you for loving me and letting me love you. Remember where ever you are I will find you. I will always Love you and I will never forget you."
See You in the Desert
My Forbidden Love
Daniel

I felt the tears slide out the corner of my eyes. I turn on my left side to smell the place he slept in. It exuded the scent of his cologne and body. I laid on it and wept like a baby. I turned over when I heard the phone.

It was Daniel, he said, "Val, is that you?" "Yes." "What are you still doing there? I thought you said you were leaving hours ago" "I tried but I couldn't let go just yet." "Babe, babe, I thought this might happen, that's why I called. Hoping you wouldn't answer the phone. But you did. I can tell you are really struggling with this.

I'm going to give you some good advice and I want you to do this follow my lead, take a hot steamy shower." "I did" "You should feel better." "I don't. Too many memories were in there." "Oh babe, I'm sorry to hear that.

Get in bed naked under your cool sheet." "I am." "Well, you should be ready to fall to sleep." "I can't the bed smells like you." "Well lay on my side of the bed. I want you to hug my pillow as if you are hugging me." "I tried that too." "Looks like the only thing left is to have that good cry you been holding back, when you cry put your face in my pillow and have a good one. What time you have to get up tomorrow? I'll call you."

"No don't. I need to do this cold turkey. Please don't call me again. Not this soon. I need to just get over the fact that you are gone. I've set my clock and packed my car. When I leave for the MOB site tomorrow I will turn everything into the main office in the morning. After I leave the MOB site I will go to my new place in Park City.

I'll get my cry out tonight but tomorrow will be the dawn of my new day." "I just want you to know, I was having the same problem but without the tears. I brought a few things that have your scent. I will hold on to them until I see you again."

"What did you take?" "Your military tee shirt and underwear." "I don't wear panties. "You do when you are in uniform; you forgot I undressed you a couple of times. I took them out of your gym bag a couple of days ago."

"You are an underwear thief." We both laughed. "No babe. I just wanted your scent."

"See I made you laugh." "I needed that and on that note, I'm going to let you go."

"You know what I think the problem is. We were together every day, for the past three weeks. I'm just having withdrawals. After Mobilization tomorrow I will be alright." "Ok, I just wanted you to know I love you and I will always hold you in my heart." "I love you and you will always be a part of my heart and soul. See you soon." "Love you."

I then hung up and laid my head on his pillow. I felt so much better since he called. I didn't feel like crying anymore. I just wanted to hold his pillow. I decided to take his pillow with me in the morning. I turned over and held his pillow and kissed it good night and fell asleep.

The next day was Mobilization day for me and my team. I got up very early when the alarm went off at 03:00 am. I jumped in the shower and took a long hot shower. I told myself this was the beginning of a new day. I thought about things I needed to do to keep myself busy starting with doing my deployment packet. I got dressed and placed everything I had to take to my new place in the trunk of my little Hoopdee.

I went up to the Penthouse and grabbed my BDU jacket and did one last walk through to see if I left anything of value. I checked my pocket for keys and Daniel's note and rubbed my fingers across the words "My Forbidden Love". I stood at the balcony window, for the very last time, and looked out at the fog which was still sitting. I said, "You're moving slow too." I looked at my watch.

I had my people to meet me at the parade field NLT 05:00. It was now 04:30. I put my lips on the sliding door window and left my lips print. I said, "Good bye, old friend you have been a comfort to me." I walked to the front door and stood, and took one last look around and with tears welling in my eyes.

I put my BDU cap on my head and slowly shut the door for the very last time. I walked down the stairs to the parking garage and got in my little convertible. I started my car and put in my cassette. Frankie Beverly was singing "It ain't Right" tears began to roll down my cheeks as I pull out my spot. I said, "When will this ever stop?" I looked in my rearview mirror for one last time as I drove towards the exit.

I dropped the keys in an envelope along with a note in the mail slot of the Tower's business office to contact me at my new address if they needed me since they already had my work number. I pulled out, from in front of the entrance and cut Frankie's cassette off. I thought to myself I remember the first day I pulled up to this place. I drove in silence, all the way to the Presidio.

When I got to the parade field two of my soldiers were there Sergeant Bigalowe and SPC Jackson. I could see there was a light up in the Command Sergeant Major's office. I said to myself *what the hell is he doing here*. I asked Sergeant Bigalowe did he know the route to Camp Parks and the detour around the Bay Bridge. He said, "Hoooah, Staff Sergeant, I recon it yesterday in my POV." I said, "Outstanding Sergeant."

My Forbidden Love

I went down to the EOC to see if there was anything there for me. Command Sergeant Major Douglas was standing at the front desk talking to the CQ. I said, "Good morning Command Sergeant Major." "Good morning Staff Sergeant Acoma." "Is there anything I can do for you CSM?" "No, I just came by to see my MOB soldiers off. I see y'all on schedule. What time you pulling out?" "In about 20 minutes at 05:30 as you directed, Command Sergeant Major.

I just have to pick something up in my office and I'll be on my way." I walked past him to my office and picked up an alert roster (which I didn't need I had one in my jacket pocket) I came out and Command Sergeant Major said, "I'll walk out with you, to see y'all off." I said, "Hoooah."

As the door closed, He asked, "How are you doing? I was a bit concerned considering the condition you left the other day." I looked at CSM and said, "I'm fine Command Sergeant Major. I had all day yesterday to get myself together and now it's all behind me and I'm ready to move on." "That's good Sergeant Acoma. I'll probably be over there about noon to see how the MOB is going." "Hoooah, Command Sergeant Major."

I walked over to Sergeant Bigalowe and handed him the alert roster and told him to do the roll call for head count. He said, "Hoooah, Staff Sergeant." (I-was-so-damn-pissed. The nerve of Command Sergeant Major! He thought I had totally fallen apart. I'm a damn Staff Sergeant not a kid out of high school). Sergeant Bigalowe called the group to fall in.

I stood off to the side as he proceeded with the roll call beginning with my name. I said "Present Sergeant". I than centered myself in front of the group and the Sergeant and asked for the report. Sergeant Bigalowe said "All present and accounted for Staff Sergeant". I told him to fall in on rank.

I put the group at ease and then gave the soldiers a safety brief about the tone of the music in the van. I expect everyone who has a cassette player to play it very low for their ears to hear only. No loud noise to distract the driver and maintain your military bearing at all time. Am I clear?"

The group yell out, **"YES STAFF SERGEANT"**. I then said, "Group attention" they came to attention. I said, "On the command fall out "Fall out and fall in on the 16 PAC, **FALL OUT."**

They did as they were directed. We headed off post toward the Bay Bridge detours as the sun began to rise. I thought to myself, ***the start of a new dawn.***

After returning from the MOB Site, I went to the new apartment in Park City. I spent most of the day arranging the apartment. My thoughts drifted off and on to Daniel. I could not help thinking about what we would be doing if he was still here. I started working on my deployment packet to forward to DA the next day.

I got up early Sunday and drove over to the Post and did my regular Sunday rituals. I ran the trail and sat out on the point and watched the cars drive across the Golden Gate Bridge. My thoughts as always drifted back to the many times we ran that trail together. I could see the hill we drove up to watch that last sunset together. ***I asked myself why is it so hard to release your thoughts from someone who means so much to you.*** I got up and ran the trail back to my car.

I got in my car and put Frankie Beverly's cassette on. I found myself taking the route across the Golden Gate Bridge. Just as I crossed the bridge I made the same turn Daniel made to Sunset Point. I parked and got out of my car and sat on the hood. I looked up the channel and watched a ship coming down the channel into the harbor. I laid back on my hood and looked up at the sky and ask, "God please release me from this feeling.

Please help me to move on" and the tears started to roll down the corner of my eyes. I said, "Help me Lord I cannot take this any longer. Why did you bring Daniel into my life and you knew I was married and thought I was in love with Christen. It just isn't fair."

I thought I was going to be strong but I am weak when it comes to how I feel about Daniel. I cannot do this alone. You are the only one that can help me. Help me Lord, help me please. My heart hurts so much." I sat up and put my hand over my face and wiped my eyes. I decided to head back across the bridge and go home. I drove back to my new apartment in silence.

The alarm went off at 0400 on Monday morning. I got up put on my PT clothes and headed for the Presidio. My thoughts drifted back again. I put Kenny G's tape in and relaxed as I drove to post.

When I got to the parking lot I met Command Sergeant Major Douglas getting out his car. He said, "Good morning Staff Sergeant Acoma. How things going? I said, "Fine Command Sergeant Major." He said, "I understand you have some changes on the alert roster. I need you to take care of that before the leader's meeting this morning."

"Hoooah Command Sergeant Major." He added, "Oh, by the way, I heard from your buddy over the weekend. He's going through his mob site now." I said, "That's really good Command Sergeant Major. I'll take care of that alert roster right away."

The meeting wasn't long. There wasn't any messages reference what was going on with the war.

I went back to the EOC and contacted Master Sergeant Davies at DA reference deployment. He answered the phone. He confirmed he had gotten a call from Sergeant First Class Jackie Taylor last week. He asked for my MOS and if I had any others, both of which I gave him.

He then told me to fax the packet to him as point of contact (POC) and he will try to work it out for me. He informed me that I will be deploying as fillers for one of the RA (regular army) units. I agreed and added that I am at this time MOB at Sixth Army EOC. He advised me to add a couple of more forms and everything else should be in the system. He promised to let me know something soon.

I faxed the packet up to him right away. When I got back to my desk, my phone was ringing. I answered, "Staff Sergeant Acoma, can I help you sir." A familiar voice said, "Yes, you can Staff Sergeant. I intoned, "**Shit**". He said, "I know what you told me, but I had to call." I said, "Call me tonight." I gave him my new home number and, told him don't you lose it. He said, "I won't." "I love you." "I love and miss you too," and hung up. When I got home, I waited anxiously for Daniel's call.

He finally called about 9:00 p.m. He said, "Hey babe, you miss me." I replied, "You know I do, how you doing?" "Great, I just wanted to hear your voice before I leave. I know it's been hard for you. You have so many things that remind you of us. I only have your scent." I laughed.

I said yesterday morning after I ran, I went to "Look out Point". I fell apart up there but I got it together." He said, "I talked to CSM, he told me, you're holding up pretty good." I said, "It's all a show." He continued, "Hang in there babe. You're strong, you've been through worse. I called to tell you, my unit is leaving for the desert on Wednesday. So in case, I didn't get to see you again, I wanted to at least hear your voice."

I said, "Well at least you have my new phone number now. I don't know how much longer, I'll be here. I sent my deployment packet to DA." He asked, "Why?" I replied, "Because this is what I want. Not so much as being near you, but because this is what I have trained so hard for, also.

Daniel, the Support Command didn't send me on all those training exercises, to sit back and watch the war on TV. I'm not scared, I want to be there." He said, "Babe this is not going to be no picnic. We are talking about a maniac who likes to play with Biological Chemicals."

I replied, "I know, but, I can handle it." He said, "Val, I don't want to sound biased, but Saudi is no place for a female, military or civilian." "I've heard that, but I can handle it." With disappointment in his voice, he said, "Well this seems like a battle I can't win." I said, "No, not this time." He said, "I guess, I see you when you get there."

He then asked, "You're not doing this because of me? So you can be near me?" Hesitantly I said, "No, according to military doctrine you'll be more in the fight than I would. I'm only combat support. You're combat arms and will be more in the fight, than me; but I do plan to be prepared." He said, "Ok, I get your point, but you be careful, be very careful, Val." "I will, just don't you worry about me. You'll have enough to worry about, like your soldiers. Don't be a Command Sergeant Major Douglas."

He then said, "I thought you two have come to somewhat of a working relationship. At least, that's what it seemed. Command

Sergeant Major said y'all talk, but you seem to be distant with your conversation.

Val, don't do this to yourself, none of this is worth you having some form of animosity, against your Command Sergeant Major. You have a damn good head on you. You should understand he did what he did for the good of everybody. You know this babe you know this.

You are about to make Sergeant First Class, and one day, you may have to make a decision like that, also. You heard him on that tape. He said women are like alligators. They'll hold on to things until the bitter end. Let it go my little alligator. You got a long ways to go. Let it go babe, let-it-go." I said, "Ok" with defeat in my voice.

He said, "I've got to go. I got some things to do before I get out of here. I'll try to give you a call before I leave on Wednesday. I Love you babe, so very much." I replied, "I love you too, Sergeant Major." He said, "You so bad; bye babe" and hung up.

I got to the office early the following morning. Since I lived further than I used to live from the Presidio, I needed to get an earlier start in the morning. I got in and checked all the incoming DA messages. There was the new list out of deploying units to the Gulf. They also had the list of soldiers to be deployed as fillers for other units. My name was not on the list.

I was a little disappointed, but I knew names don't show on the list until the "Warning Orders" has been cut. Once the warning has gone out, the initial mobilization order is issued to the unit or the individual. After completion of mobilization processing the individual's deployment order is cut along with the unit notification of departure.

There were two soldiers from the EOC in the Regular Army who were on the list, Staff Sergeant Jackson and SPC Brown they both held the 88M MOS and had military driver's licenses. CSM came down and said, Staff Sergeant Acoma, I assume you are aware we are losing two of the EOC personnel. I said, "Yes Command Sergeant Major." "I would need you to step up and cover both teams temporarily as NCOIC. I said, "Yes, Command Sergeant Major."

He continued, "You are the most knowledgeable person when it comes to running the EOC. We are losing people every day because of this Build up, even though it is to be expected. We have to move people where they are the best asset. That is why COL Everett and I have decided to put you in charge of both shifts. You will temporarily work both shifts, on a split shift basis.

You will work out a plan to adjust your work schedule to meet the mission requirement. Once you have come up with that plan, I need you to discuss it with me, and I would then be the approving authority. Understand this Staff Sergeant Acoma; this is a temporary fix to a temporary manpower problem. I said, "Hoooah, Command Sergeant Major, that's an easy fix, when will this all take effect?" "As soon as we can get the schedule worked out."

I worked out a schedule where I would work the early parts of both shift. I told Command Sergeant Major what I had decided, he agreed with it. He said, "That seems most reasonable. I think Monday is the best time to begin that new work schedule. Friday will be Staff Sergeant Jackson's last day with us. I know you two been briefing each other on the mission. She needs to get you caught up before her departure." I said, "I'll get with her before the days' out."

Jackie called me and told me she was leaving for the Gulf on Friday. I told her I had sent Master Sergeant Davies my packet and he was working it. She asked, "Sergeant Major Howard deployed yet? I told her, "He's leaving Fort Lewis on Wednesday. He'll be there before you get there. That means you'll spend Christmas in Saudi." She said, "I guess." I asked her was she scared. "No just anxious. It's the waiting that's getting to me.

How you handling Daniel's leaving? You two were regular 'two love birds'. I could see there was more than friendship. There was a lot of love between you two." "You right a lot of love. It was pretty rough for a while there, but I'm getting better."

"When I get there, I'll look him up." "Thanks, who knows, I maybe there before you know it." She said, "I'll be there. I'll see you when you get there." I warned, "Be careful and don't be no hero." She said, "You know me I always know how to get out of a mess." I said, "Ok Jackie, Bye." "Bye Val. See you in the desert." We hung up.

My phone rang about two in the morning. I pondered, who could that be? I heard that familiar deep voice say hey babe it's me. I asked, "What time is it?" "It's about two o'clock, Wednesday morning. I called you to tell you in about two hours we are wheels up. This was my only opportunity to call before we left. I just wanted you to know I love and miss you so very much." I replied, "I love and miss you too".

"Just remember everything I said and maybe we will see each other over here." I said, "Just remember a lot of people are depending on you so, don't be no hero except mine's." "Well, on that note I'm going to say bye, and I love you and I always will." "I love you too," and hung up. I said a brief prayer and asked God to keep him safe and fell back to sleep.

Things stayed pretty normal around the EOC. Jackson left for deployment and I worked the split shift. About two weeks later Staff Sergeant Johnson was assigned as Staff Sergeant Jackson's replacement. I was glad. Working those two split shifts was having its toll on me. Things would get back to normal. I hadn't heard from Jackie or Daniel since they left.

Christmas was coming in a few days I had decided not to go home for Christmas, but I did put up a Christmas tree in the apartment. I bought a really nice one and put it up in front of the big picture window in the living room. I had talked to Christen often and more than we had when I was at the Penthouse. He said he was coming up for the holidays.

I got a call the following day from Master Sergeant Davies from DA. He said, "Sergeant Acoma, well you got what you wanted. You have deployment orders for the Saudi Arabia." I asked, "Where I'm going?" "The 2nd Aviation Battalion, 2nd Armor Division out of Fort Hood, Texas. You'll be assigned to their PAC as their Redeployment NCO." He continued, "Let me fill you in on a little secret about these filler positions.

As a reservist they will have some animosity toward you because they think you are not as good as regular Army. Don't let that hinder you from doing your job.

Do not at any time let on that you are a reservist because they will try to treat you as one. Regular Army has little or no respect for what they call "Weekend Warriors". You must show them you are a soldier and a damn good one. That's all I have to say about that.

When you get in country look up your girl Taylor she's assigned to a Regular Army Movement Control unit out of El Paso, TX. I sent her an email and told her you have a MOB date of 7 January 1991. So good luck Staff Sergeant and don't be NO hero." "Thanks a lot Master Sergeant." "Again Good Luck Staff Sergeant Acoma, and God Speed." We hung up.

The next day I got to the EOC the CQ said the Command Sergeant Major came down looking for you, I told him you haven't gotten in yet. He said when you get in, he needs to see you. I said Hoooah!

I went into my office and searched through the orders and the call up list and there it was: *"Staff Sergeant Valeria B. Acoma" you are hereby notified as a designated mobilization soldier; as support personnel to Operation Desert Shield/Desert Storm" Your unit of Assignment is the 2nd Aviation Battalion, 2nd Armor Division, Fort Hood, TX with effective date of 7 January 1991." This is a warning order to make you aware of getting your personal affairs in order. "Mobilization Order" will immediately follow.*

I made a copy of the Warning order and put it in my jacket pocket and went up to see the Command Sergeant Major. It was still early. Command Sergeant Major was sitting at his desk as I walked in and knocked on his door. He said, "Come in Staff Sergeant Acoma *(It's always business when he calls your full rank and name)*, I guess you know you came up on the list." "Yes Command Sergeant Major." "It never fails, they always call the best, and you are among the best Sergeant Acoma.

I just wanted to talk to you before you get out of here and I miss the opportunity. He went on to say, "I know things have been somewhat rocky a few months back, but I hope that is all behind us. I make no excuses, but I just want you to know, I felt I did what I had to do for all parties involved and their careers. I mean yours Sergeant Acoma, Dan's and mine. We all will come out ahead whether you know it or not." "I know Command Sergeant Major I truly know it was for the better."

"Sergeant when you get over there. Don't go looking for him. Let him find you. He is now a Command Sergeant Major in charge of over 2,000 man ordnance battalion. He has a huge responsibility and he does not need any type of disruption. By the time you get over there, the **"SHIT"** would have just hit the fan, and his soldiers would be a huge part of it.

Let me give you some damn good advice. You are a reservist, but don't go telling anyone that, in the unit you are going to. You have been here on active duty so long you carry yourself, as a Regular Army soldier.

Continue to do that. If anyone asked you where you were assigned you tell them HQ Sixth Army, Presidio San Francisco. It would not be a lie. You are very aware of how Regular Army treats reservist and national guards, although some are even better soldiers.

I know you are going to do well, and you will be promotable. Have you been to Advance Non-commissioned Officer Course (ANCO)?" "Yes, Command Sergeant Major two years ago, the CG had me placed in "Fast Track"." "That's great, that mean, you had someone looking out for your career. Many soldiers don't have that. They try to do it on their own. All soldiers need a mentor. You Sergeant Acoma are a very good mentor.

One day you'll make First Sergeant and a damn good one, but you have to always remember your soldiers come first. From what I can tell and see you're already doing that." He concluded and said, "I just wanted to give you some insight before you get so caught up in your deployment, we'll talk again." "Hoooah Command Sergeant Major," and got up and left.

The word swept through the EOC like wild fire that I was deploying. I called Christen when I got home and told him I was deploying. He said, "Well, it's not like it wasn't something we weren't expecting. What you going to do about your apartment?" "I don't know my MOB date is 7 January 1991. I should fly out of Fort Dix about 12 January 1991.

I told my landlord I was getting deployed. I might have to move out. I would let them know what my plans are. They told me they have a lot of soldiers deployed and kept their apartment. I could do the same."

I decided to not go home for the Christmas holiday. Christen came up I had not seen him in so long. I was so happy to see my husband. I met him at the airport. I let him drive back to my apartment. He said my car was just what I needed small and economical. I think it would be a perfect idea to keep your apartment while you were deployed.

I can come up often and check on it. He would have a place to go to get away from LA. *(I thought, now he needs a place to go, just to get away from LA, after I get deployed, but not when I was living here.)* "I would appreciate that and I'll leave my car so you can get around."

He said, he may have his sister and brother-in-law come up when they come in town. I told him that's up to you just take care of my place. You know the Army's is paying for it. I gave him a set of keys to the apartment. I asked, "So, how is your apartment." He said, "It was nice but it wasn't nice as this one."

We went out to dinner at a nice restaurant at the "Fisherman's Wharf". I made sure we didn't go to places Daniel and I had gone. We made a lot of love that weekend. I really missed my husband. We brought the New Year in together with a bottle of Champagne and a lot of love making.

On New Years' day Christen said he had to get back to Los Angeles. It was hard to let him go, but I had to start getting ready to deploy. I told him to give me a call when he got back to LA. He called me the next day.

I needed to out process out of Sixth Army. I had notified my landlord I was going to keep my apartment and I had someone to look after it. They said it was not a problem but I had to put his name on an access card in the office.

The days drew closer for my departure for deployment. I talked to Command Sergeant Major several times since he first got word. They had an award ceremony as they always had for deploying soldiers. I got an Army Commendation Medal (ARCM). I signed out the unit for the final time.

I then called Debbie back at the Support Command and told her I was deploying in a couple of days. She said they got the word when they received a copy of my orders from DA. Val, you be careful." I said, "I will and thanks for everything." She said, "She would sign me out the unit on deployment that way when you come back all you have to do is sign back in." I told her thanks again for everything.

The day I left for Fort Dix, I parked my little car in the apartment parking garage and left my keys in the apartment. I then caught a super shuttle to the airport. When I got to the airport I gave Christen a call, to let him know I was leaving and where I had left everything.

I was shocked he answered the phone. He sounded very sleepy. He asked could I call him back later. He just got in from driving his cab all night. I asked was he going to be there because I really needed to talk to him. He said, "Um hm." I said, "Ok bye, I love you." He said, "Bye, I love you too."

I didn't get to talk to Christen for three days after many times trying to get him on the phone. All it was doing was just ringing. I finally got him early one morning. He said he was sorry. He had gotten all my messages. I told him I just wanted to hear his voice before I left. We were flying out late that night and I did not know when I would be able to talk with him again.

It finally dawned on me, Christen and I was growing apart in totally different directions. I had no idea what he was into but he knew everything about me, almost. I knew he was hiding something, but I was in no position, to try and find out.

Plus it was not in me to try and keep up with him. In another 24 hours I would be on the other side of the world; preparing for a war none of us knew what the outcome will be. This was not the time or place to worry about what Christen was into.

CHAPTER Twelve

Wheels up for our flight were 02:00 from Newark International Airport. The flight was a sixteen hour flight across the Atlantic Ocean into Dhahran Military Airfield in Saudi Arabia.

We arrived in Saudi Arabia airspace about 01:00 on the 11th of January 1991. The pilot came on the speaker and said, "From this moment all passengers will need to pull the blinds down on the windows next to them and any seat where there is a seat without a person occupying it. Keep all blinds down until told to do so after the flight lands.

No pictures will be taken once we land and deplaned the aircraft. Everyone will remain in their seat until otherwise told different." His last words were, "Welcome to the "United Emirate of Saudi Arabia; and may God be with you".

Once we landed, the Host Nation Representative came on the plane and gave us some specific information. The Representative was an American speaking person who looked of Arabic descent. He said "Welcome to the United Emirate of Saudi Arabia.

You are guest of a country that is of Islamic belief. It is our responsibility to respect our host and their beliefs. At this time I will ask you to pull down all sleeves and cover heads at your host request. It is 02:00 hours in the morning Saudi time and the temperature here on the Tarmac is 102 degrees. It gets up to 120 to 130 degrees here in

Saudi on a daily basis. You must keep yourself hydrated at all times. So drink a lot of water and keep your extra water on hand at all times. Dehydration can be deadly if not taken seriously.

As you deplane, stay between the yellow lines on the ground and follow in a straight line behind the person in front of you. Once inside the building you will be briefed on other information and inprocessed. Once you have inprocessed you will meet up with a representative from your assigned unit and escorted to their area. Again welcome to the United Emirate of Saudi Arabia and keep hydrated."

After all the briefs and inprocessing I was met by my unit's representative, Staff Sergeant Janet Mason. Staff Sergeant Mason was NCOIC of the admin section to 2nd Aviation Battalion. She was the Duty NCO for the Battalion. It was about 03:00 when we got to "Khobar Towers" where the military and civilians were housed.

Khobar Towers was a housing complex built by the Saudis near the city of Dhahran, Eastern Province, Saudi Arabia, but were unoccupied until the Gulf War in 1990. The complex living quarters were high-rise apartments up to eight stories tall and included office space and administrative facilities; mainly as a transition point for incoming and outgoing military personnel. The underground parking area was converted into a multinational dining facility; which was open 24 hours for all personnel because of the duty requirements.

I was given temporary quarters until the next day. Staff Sergeant Mason said she would be back about 0730 to take me to my duty section. She asked me would I need a wakeup call. I said, "I might, just in case." "I'll send my runner over to make sure you're up."

There was like a six hour difference between here and the east coast and nine hours between the west coast." "Thanks for the information." *(I thought to myself now I'm really mentally screwed up)* She had showed me where the dining facilities just in case I got hungry. I was still suffering from Jet Lag. So I decided to walk over to the dining facilities instead, and get some coffee or hot chocolate.

It had been a while since I ate in one. According to Sergeant Mason everyone ate in the dining hall instead on the economy, mainly because the food was much better. I walked in the building and I heard a voice say "Staff Sergeant Acoma". I looked around and it was SPC, Walker from the Support Command. He said, "Staff Sergeant Umm, Outstanding how the hell are you?" I said, "Great SPC Walker, it's always good to see a familiar face, in an unfamiliar place."

As we walked through the line to get some breakfast, He asked, "When did you get here?" I told him, "About four hours ago." "And you aren't sleepy?" "No, not yet, I'm still suffering from Jet Lag." "Yeah, it'll take a while to get adjusted, and it's like nine hours yesterday, in Los Angeles. But don't worry you'll catch on."

He then said, "I see your buddy Sergeant First Class Jackie Taylor, is here also." "Yeah, I know I really need to find her."

"She works for the "Host Nations Support" Section over where all the United Nation Big Wheels are. She's got it made. She usually comes through here about this time every morning for breakfast." I said, "I might just wait around, and see if I can catch her." He said, "I don't work too far from here, if I see her, I'll let her know you're 'In Country'." I said, "Thanks Walker, I really appreciate that."

I ate a little breakfast but didn't want to get full because I didn't want to fall asleep when I got back to my room. As I walked down the walkway to my building, I heard a very familiar female, voice say, "Staff Sergeant Valeria B. Acoma", I knew right away who it was. I turned around and said "Sergeant First Class Jackie Taylor", I know, that voice anywhere. We hugged so tight; my best friend in this world.

She said, "It's about time." I said, "Well, I made it. I got to get back, I haven't gotten to my unit yet and I don't have quarters either." "I saw your man; I told him you were on your way here." I asked, "So, how he looked?" "Girrl, that man looked damn good. You know, he's a Command Sergeant Major, now. So, you've got to behave yourself." "I know."

She then said, "Here's my number, call me when you get settled. You know the 'Shit is about to hit the Fan'." I said, "I heard." She added, "His people are headed north in a couple of days. They're going to be right in the middle of it." I said, "I've got to go. I'll let you know where I'm staying and working." We hugged and said, see you later.

I walked back to my quarters and saw Sergeant Mason going into my building. I called out to her, and told her I went to get some breakfast. She said, "Oh, no problem, we're still a little early. We can go over to where you will be working and then to the Company to in process you. Did you get any sleep?" "No, I was scared I would over sleep, so I went to the dining facilities."

"I did the same thing, when I got here. The only problem is that when you do crash, you're going to be out for a while. That "Jet Lag" really sucks maybe you might get some time to get settled in before things starts heating up out there." I said, "I hope so."

The 2nd Aviation was located on the King Khalid air base. Our battalion was located off in a building near the helicopters' hangar. It was getting hot on the airbase, and it was still early morning. When we got there, the battalion's Sergeant Major Brown was there. He said, "Staff Sergeant Acoma, glad to see you made it, before things started really getting hot up north.

Come on in my office, I talked with your Command Sergeant Major from Sixth Army DCOPS. He speaks very highly of you. I understand you ran the headquarters EOC during some very critical periods. I said, "If you referring to the earthquake, yes I did Sergeant Major. He said, "So, when you hear artillery fire and Jets taking off you should be alright." (*I thought what that's got to do with the EOC).*

As the Sergeant Major it is my responsibility to give you a little history of this unique unit. If you didn't notice, this unit wears their combat patch over their heart not on their right shoulder arm as other units does.

As a matter of fact the 2nd Armor division is the only unit in the United States Army that does. It goes back when General Patton was the Division Commander, at that time he was just a Colonel Patton.

Well, it is said, that the unit was so dear to his heart he requested that the division could wear the division patch over their heart and not their sleeves. His unit was given that privilege. When he died the unit continued to wear the patch over their heart as a request from his wife.

The unit was deactivating when it got called for Operation Desert Shield/Storm. It will continue to wear its combat patch over its heart until deactivation. It will then be moved to the right arm as a combat patch. So, if anyone ask you why, the 2nd Armor wear's it patch over its heart tell them because "the unit was dear to General Patton's heart". It is one of the proudest or if not the proudest units in the United States Army.

We have a custom here in 2nd Aviation battalion; everyone who comes into the battalion will go on a maiden helicopter mission. I said, "Oh that's great." "Have you ever been on one before?" I said, "Yes, Sergeant Major (I lied)." He said, "Then you'll be just fine. Master Sergeant Lewis, the Master Crew Chief will set that up." "Hoooah, Sergeant Major."

He then said, "Now, We need to get you settled in, before you fall out on your feet. You look exhausted." "I am a little tired. I haven't been to sleep yet. He then said, "Once we get you over to the HHC and get you signed in and your quarters assigned, I'll give you some time to get some sleep and settled in." "Thanks Sergeant Major."

He continued, "Oh, by the way there was a Command Sergeant Major Howard, that came by. He said y'all worked together at Sixth Army. I told him you haven't reported in yet. He said he'll try to catch you before his unit moves north." I said, "Thank you, Sergeant Major."

"In the meanwhile let me show you where you will be working and then I'll take you over to HHC and get you processed in. You'll be working in the redeployment with the PAC section. Master Sergeant Lacy will be the NCOIC. She will be your immediate supervisor. She will let you know what your responsibility will be. They all should be in about an hour, they had PT this morning. In the meanwhile, let me get you over to HHC and get you settled in."

I processed into HHC and got my building and room number at Khobar Towers. I shared the room with three other NCOs in the unit. Sergeant Major told me once I get processed I could have the rest of the day off so I could get some sleep and settled in. I unpacked and made my bunk. I laid down and slept for about six hours until I heard the other females coming into the room trying to be quiet.

The other females in my room were all Staff Sergeant, James, Mason and Jamison from 2nd Armor Division. They asked me if I was hungry because they were going to the dining facility. I said I would walk over later. Soon after they left I heard a knock on my door. It was Jackie. I asked, "How did you find me?" "I called your unit. I'm on my dinner hour and I thought you might be hungry."

"Give me a minute and I'll walk over with you." So, you're over at the airfield." "Yeah where it is very noisy and very Regular Army." "I know that's not going to bother you. You've been on tour so long, you're just like RA." "I know it doesn't matter. It's just a matter of speaking. As a matter of fact, I am a little hungry."

We got in line and got our food. We found a table and sat down to eat. I was sitting with my back to the entrance. I saw Jackie stand and said, "Well long time no see, Command Sergeant Major."

I heard a very familiar deep voice say, "What's up Sergeant First Class, Jackie Taylor," I turned my head and looked to the end of the table. I said, "Well, I'll be Command Sergeant Major, Howard." He smiled and winked, "Staff Sergeant Valeria B. Acoma." I shook his hand. (I've never shook his hand before) I said, "Congratulations on your promotion." He asked, "Is this table taken?" We said, "No, please." Jackie said, "I've got to get back, I have the late shift tonight." "Acoma can you find your way back?" CSM said, "I'll walk her back." Jackie said, "I'll catch you later."

Daniel said, "Damn you look good in your Tri-colors." "You look damn good yourself, Command Sergeant Major." He said, "I guess, we really have to play the role now." I smiled and said, "Sure you right." "I didn't know how I would react, when I saw you." I suggested, "Lets walk and talk, it's a little crowded and loud in here."

"Good idea. What time you got to get back?" "I'm off until tomorrow I'm trying to get settled in." "You got here just in time I'm headed up north to KKMC in two days. The ground war starts about then."

We had made it back to my building; we sat on the concrete barriers in front of the building. Daniel stopped and said, "Damn, I missed you so much, babe. I think about you all the time." He then stood with his arms folded with authority, smiled and said, "I told you, I would find you" and gave me that famous wink. I smiled and said,

"Yes you did, and you did." He said, "I Love you so much. I've wanted to say that since I saw you and Jackie sitting at the table.

Have you gotten settled in yet?" "Kind of, I'm still trying to get over the Jet Lag." "A little secret, I found helpful. You still taking B12 and B6?" "Yeah, but I haven't lately." "I'm surprised, that doesn't sound like you. Well, they really help to get you back on track. Just take one instead of two.

Make sure you drink a lot of water and keep hydrated. You will not know when you are dehydrated. I've had several cases a day with soldiers not drinking enough water. Once you start getting real bad stomach cramps you have gone too long. Water's not going to help. You are going to need a "Saline Drip" through "IV". It's not a good feeling to be dehydrated. So drink your water babe, whether you want it or not."

I said, "It's so good to hear you call me that." He said, "I can't spend much time with you now, but when we come back out of the desert, I can make time for you. It won't be long, but it will be valuable time. I just wish we could spend some personal time together. I just miss, holding you so much." I said, "I miss you holding me, too."

"Well Val, you got what you wanted, and it's not going to be fun and games. In a few days who knows we'll be in the middle of an all and out war, with a crazy man. To be perfectly honest! I didn't want you here, and for you to be on that airfield, in Dhahran, that's not the safest place to be, either. You just be careful. I mean it Val, be very damn careful. You are so damn head strong. I love you babe, and I don't want to lose you, especially not to this war."

I said, "I'm going to be alright honey; I didn't come here for you to worry about me. I don't want you to either, but I know you will. Daniel, you're a Command Sergeant Major now, you know that's a huge responsibility. So you make sure you stay focused as always, Daniel, go take care of your business and soldiers. I'll be right here when you come back from up north. I'm not going anywhere, I just got here."

He said, "Well, I got to get back; you just remember everything I told you. Drink a lot of water and be careful. I'll try to see you before

I leave, but if I don't, you know I love you babe." "I love you too; and don't be No hero. As he walked away, arrogantly he said, I'm already a hero. I said, "Hoooah, Command Sergeant Major."

When I got back to my room there was a note on the door for me. It was from Master Sergeant Lacy telling me what time my ride to the work area would pick me up in the morning. I went in my room and took a warm shower and got ready for bed.

I was still trying to figure out the time back in LA. I really needed to talk to Christen. I set my alarm so I didn't over sleep and laid back on my bunk and thought about the past minutes I spent with Daniel. I then dozed off.

CHAPTER

Fourteen

The Unit had a "Haji Bus" that picked us up every morning after chow to take us up to the airfield. I had gotten a little familiar with my duty responsibility. I handle all movement of battalion size units to the "forward" and back to home station redeployment of all and any personnel. The job was pretty much the same as I was doing at Sixth Army, but instead of over 30,000 soldiers.

I had only a battalion sized unit of about 1,000 soldiers. Master Sergeant Lacy and I had established a pretty good working relationship. Our office was a busy place. People were in and out all the time. I heard Master Sergeant Lacy call "At Ease" and every soldier and I, in the room came to their feet. My work area was behind a partition behind Master Sergeant Lacy desk. I heard her say good morning Command Sergeant Major can I help you with anything?

I heard that familiar deep voice say, "Yeah, Master Sergeant. I understand you have a Staff Sergeant Acoma working here." She said, "Yes, Command Sergeant Major." He said, "I used to work with her, back at Sixth Army, mind if I speak to her for a moment, my unit is about to head north." She said, "Sure Command Sergeant Major, not a problem." When I heard his voice, I had stepped from behind my partition. I said, "Command Sergeant Major Howard." He said, "Staff Sergeant Acoma." We shook hands and we then walked outside.

He said, as we walked down the safe side of the yellow line on the airfield, "I had to make a point to see you before I left, babe."

My Forbidden Love

"I thought you had left." "My main body pulled out at 04:00 this morning. I have some soldiers that are here in the hospital. I'm going to check on their status and move out maybe later today.

"One of your implied duties huh" "That's what I do, take care of my soldiers," "And that you do, including me." He smiled and said, "You're one of my soldiers', I am a Command Sergeant Major." "And they thought you wouldn't make it." "I talked to Tom. He knows it" "Good!"

"I wanted to make sure everything is alright with you. The ground war is, going to start in a few days. It's not going to be pretty." "I'm going to be alright. I've got God on my side." "I'm sure you do. If we play this thing right it won't take long, hopefully it'll be over before you know it."

"I hope so. It may even be a little quiet around here since most of the units have moved forward but, not here on the airfield. It's getting really busy around here." He commented, "I see, they're convoying that heavy artillery to load on those fly missions."

"I was told they've been doing that for about a week. I guess it's really going to happen." "Yea, it is babe; it's going to be a lot of fireworks. I mean lots of fireworks, and it's not like the Fourth of July," he continued, "There's going to be a lot of noise coming from about 100 miles away; but it's going to sound very close, because there is nothing but desert and lots of open space especially when those planes start taking off and returning. Those fly overs are very loud."

He concluded, "Well, I've got to get going and check on those soldiers." "You keep safe, Hero," I said. This time he gave me a big tight hug. He whispered in my ear "damn I love you, lady" "I love you too, my darling" He said "I don't want to let you go" I responded, "me either." We let go of each other. He added, "Stay safe for me, if not for you." "Go get 'em hero. See you later Command Sergeant Major." He said, "Me too" and we both walked in opposite directions.

When I got back to the office, Master Sergeant Lacy said, "That's a fine looking, Command Sergeant Major." I said, "He is; he's like a big brother to me." She commented, "He looks mighty young for a Command Sergeant Major." "You know how those Combat Arms units are. He's an Ordnance Command Sergeant Major." She asked, "Where are they headed?" "Somewhere called Emerald City near KKMC," I said. MSG Lacy then said, "They must be part of the forward elements." I replied, "I guess so." (*I said to myself why did she tell me that, now I really got to pray, I said, God please keep him and his soldiers safe*).

It was really busy around the airfield the next few days. The entrance to the airbase, where we worked was blocked every morning by the long convoys of flatbeds bringing ordnance in for the air strikes. We had to walk about a mile from the front gate to our building.

Master Sergeant Lacy told us, "Once they launched the air attack we will do a stand down. We might move over to one of the offices at Khobar Towers until after the air attack has ceased fire. Otherwise we'll continue to work here until we are given the order to "Stand Down".

Intelligence had the airstrike to begin on the 17th of January. On the day before the air attack, was scheduled to be launched we were given the "Stand Down" order. We were directed to move all equipment and documents to a building down in Khobar Towers away from the airfield. Intelligence said there was a possibility of "SCUD" attacks near the Dhahran and King Khalid airfield.

Outside of the security barriers at Khobar Towers' housing complex had become "Media City", just outside the entrances. There were trailers and masses of GP large tents stretched as far as the eyes could see for the news media from all around the world. We were given strict orders not to, at any time, talk to any of the media for any reason.

They would call to us as we entered the complex. They would line up along the concrete barriers with their cameras and microphones with their station call signs displayed on their microphone. They were not allowed to come within fifty feet of the Serpentine barricades.

The Media Camp, as we called it, was guarded by the Coalition Security Guards to keep the peace among the media people. They had their own Mess Tent and a huge circus tent for daily briefings by

My Forbidden Love

the Coalition Forces Commander, General Schwarzkopf's, Deputy Commander, Lieutenant General Waller and others on his staff.

General Schwarzkopf was a very tall and huge burley like white man who stood about six foot five. I had the honor of meeting him on several occasions before the war. He was often at the Pentagon at meetings with General Thurman the VCSA and the CSA, General Wickham. Also when the IX Corp' Corp's Support Command had their annual Command and Control Conference (C3) at the Los Angeles Air Station, he was the I CORP Commander at that time. He attended the conference. I was working the sign-in table.

He asked, "Where have I seen you before?" I stood and said I used to work for the VCSA, General Thurman when you used to attend several of the meets on the "E" ring. He said oh yeah "Mad Max". I smiled and said, "Yes sir." He said, "Good seeing you again." He had a distinct thing about never forgetting a face. General Schwarzkopf, as the CORP Commander and Lt General Waller, as his deputy commander at that time, were at I Corp when I participated in several of the CORP'S exercises.

General Schwarzkopf had a deep concerned for the soldiers fighting the war. He felt the so called, "Chocolate Chips" uniforms were not good for those soldiers in the desert. They were very uncomfortable as well as the material they were made of, that is why they came up with the TRI-color uniforms; which were cooler and more ventilated. The desert boots were also a problem for the fighting soldiers in the desert. They had no ventilation and were uncomfortable around the calves and shins.

General Schwarzkopf had DA issue the "Tri-color" and the desert boots with ventilation and padding around the calves and shins on the desert boots. DA called them Schwarzkopf boots which became initial issue for all deploying soldiers.

Later that night about one in the morning, we heard the first air strike fly overs take off from King Khalid airbase. Many of us went out in the complex parking lot and watched and listened for the jets taking off. Even though they were about twenty miles away, they could be heard.

The Media Camp had satellite dish placed throughout the camp for broadcasting throughout the world. CNN had the largest satellite dish where other stations were bouncing off theirs.

We could get CNN broadcasting where they had several of their reporters in Bagdad during the initial air attacks. We watched the voice commentator give a play by play of each attack.

The air strikes went on for about several weeks; pounding on various targets in the city of Bagdad. Then on 23 February 1991 word came down that the ground war was going to start the next day. To us back in the rear, at Khobar Towers we knew this probably meant that whatever happened, it would happen early in the morning while it was still dark in Bagdad and Kuwait City.

We watched from the parking lots where large TV Monitors were set up by CNN so we could watch back in the rear. We could hear artillery echoing throughout the desert in the distant. The sound of ordnance going off interrupted the coverage on the screen from the satellite dish. Although it was further north, we could feel it down in Khobar as if it was an earthquake.

Most of us were not able to sleep during that time, with sirens warning of possible SCUD attacks. I only knew of one that got close to Khobar Towers but was destroyed by the Patriots which stood guard around the complex.

Soldiers that were on SCUD watch listened for the sound of each artillery round. The Patriots stood ready, as we watched on a giant Jumbo-vision TV screen, the final battle of the war. There had been no SCUD attacks since the devastating incident that killed the National Guards soldiers on the airfield a few days back. The explosion and shelling went on for hours all through the next two days as the sun came up.

I prayed that Daniel was nowhere near what was going on up north. I knew his soldiers were involved in a lot of the ordnance that were being used and exploding.

Then on 26 February, there were a lot of jets doing low flyovers heading north as they were taking off from the airfield. We got word that the Iraqi had bombed the Kuwaiti oil fields as a decoy just north of the Kuwait City along Highway 80 leading to Bagdad.

Some of the Iraqis that were in Kuwaiti new leadership, put in place by Saddam Hussein, were trying to escape back to Bagdad but US Coalition Forces jets took them out along the highway 80 stretch to the Iraqi/Kuwaiti border; just north of KKMC.

On the morning of 27 February, 1991 word got out that the coalition forces had taken back Kuwait City. There were cheers from the apartment building complex, parking lot out in the Media Camp. It was like a carnival in Khobar Towers. Everyone was waiting for the word from President Bush on the cease fire.

According to the Coalition Commander General Schwarzkopf, we had met our objective, which was to take back Kuwait City from the Iraqi dictator Saddam Hussein. President Bush called cease fire on 27 February 1991. The cease-fire took effect 08:00 hours the following morning,

After all the fighting was over, our section moved back to the air base, our main responsibility was redeployment and sustainment. On our third day back at the airfield, Master Sergeant Lacy asked, "Staff Sergeant Acoma have you been on your maiden flight yet?" I said, "No, Master Sergeant."

She said, "Well you're up for the next flight, going out on a humanitarian, search and rescue mission. It's not bad, could be a lot of fun. You need to report over to the helicopter hangar, at 07:30 tomorrow, to the Master Crew Chief, Master Sergeant Lewis. He's good people and his people will treat you right.

When I got back at the room that night, Staff Sergeant Mason said, "Acoma, I heard you going on your maiden flight in the morning." I said, "Yeah." She said, "Look girlfriend, I'm going to be perfectly honest with you, those helicopter pilots like to screw around with the newbie up there."

"Some good advice, keep that shoulder and waist harness on tight, and don't eat any breakfast; their intension is to make you lose it." I asked, "Why they do that?" "It breaks the monotony, but don't let them get to you." "Thanks, for the warning. So, no one was going to tell me." She said, "No, they did everyone like that." I couldn't do anything but shake my head and said, "I'm going to be alright."

I reported to the hangar at 07:00. Master Sergeant Lewis was already there. He said, "So, Staff Sergeant Acoma you ready to take that first flight in an 'Apache'." I said, "Yes, Master Sergeant." He said, "Ok, we'll see." Thinking *(Now that was a real sign they were going to screw around up there.)*

He said, "All you'll be doing is looking out the side doors for stranded Iraqi soldiers. They might be "Kurds" or part of the "Iraqi military" that got separated from their units. We drop leaflets and let them know the war is over.

We let them know they are now POWs, and according to the "Geneva Convention," they will be fed, clothed and treated humanely. They must present a white flag of surrender or the shirt off their back as a sign of surrender.

We usually drop bottles of water and MREs in case they are thirsty or hungry. We radio back to the command and give coordinates of their location and they will be apprehended or picked up.

He continued, "We're usually out there about an hour to an hour and a half. Go use the latrine we'll lift off in 20 minutes." I said, "Yes Master Sergeant, will you be going?" He said, "Yeah, I always go on those maiden flights."

I went to the Latrine. Master Sergeant Lewis said, "Let's get a move on. Our bird is at the end of the runway. You're not nervous are you?" *(Like saying you look nervous)* I said, "No, Master Sergeant, I'm alright." I put my earplugs in as we drove down the airfield.

When we got to the helipad, he explained, "We always do a safety brief and safety check before liftoff. Always remember to hold on to that handrail just above your head and the door. Do not hang out the doors at any time. If you spot any ground movement use the clock signs from right to left.

The pilot will maneuver in that direction. Do a constant safety check on your waist and shoulder harness. This is for your own safety. On lift off, stand clear of the door with your back, against the rear side panel. Enjoy your ride."

Master Sergeant Lewis put on his ear phone and said, "Ok, Chief it's a lift off." The helicopter lifted a little off the airfield and went straight across the airfield. I clung to the wall like Velcro on that take off. Master Sergeant Lewis turned and looked at me and said, "You alright over there Sergeant Acoma." I said, Hoooah, Master Sergeant."

That thing was moving fast. He said, "Come over here Sergeant Acoma, that's why I'm here. I'm not going to let anything happen to you." He then said, "This bird is known as the helicopters race horse, its fast and it's quiet. You can't hear it, coming when it's coming.

We're going north east just parallel to highway 80 towards KKMC and the Kuwait-Iraq border; and then swing back off 80 going south and circle around to check that bombed out area near the Kuwait oil fires. Then back to the airfields. It's a short trip so hold on and enjoy the ride." I said, "Hoooah, Master Sergeant."

As we headed north there was a possible sighting at one o'clock near the Iraqi border. Master Sergeant Lewis explained, "Notice the head dress, those are Kurds trying to make it back to the north east border. They're no threat. They're heading home." It was about six of them. They were waving their shirts and motions with their hands towards their mouth for water.

The pilot swooped lower to get a closer look. I felt like I died, I held on for dear life. Everyone else was calm. Lewis told the other crew chief, "Drop them a box of those MREs and a case of water." "They got the fighting over the water and MREs." They waved, and we raced across the desert going north. That bird was fast, but smooth.

We then saw a sighting at about 12 o'clock of about ten soldiers running when they got sight of us coming. Lewis said, "They maybe royal guards. Their uniforms are mixed match." The pilot did a bank right and swooped down on top of them. They all fell to their knees with their weapons over their heads. The pilot did several circle turns around them and I lost the little bit of orange juice, I had for breakfast on the floor.

The other crew chief asked, "Staff Sergeant, you didn't eat any breakfast? I didn't see any Chunks come up." I wanted to tell him

"Kiss my Ass". I said, "I'm not a breakfast person. "(I lied) Master Sergeant Lewis told them in Arabic, "Put your weapons down. You are now Prisoners of War." They started cheering. (They were happy) Master Sergeant Lewis said, "That happens all the time. They're ready to give up. He told them to sit there and we'll be back."

We threw some leaflets down to them, a case of MREs and a case of water; the other crew chief radioed in the coordinates for the MPs to apprehend the POWs. When we left, they were laying back drinking water and eating MREs. They then waved bye to us. I thought to myself some POWs.

The pilot banks left and headed south towards the airfield. I was so glad. Another one of those sighting, and I would have had to change my underwear before going back to work.

We got back about 10:30. Master Sergeant Lewis said, "Staff Sergeant Acoma, you did outstanding. You didn't even lose your breakfast." I smiled and said, "Only some of it." He laughed and said, "Good job." I said, "Thanks, Master Sergeant" and went back to my office.

When I got back to my office, Master Sergeant Lacy asked, "How was the mission?" I said, "It went great. We cornered about ten Iraqi soldiers, trying to get back across the border and some Kurds trying to get to the North east.

All in all, it was a successful mission." One of the soldiers asked, "Did you get sick Staff Sergeant?" I replied, "Not really, I only had orange juice for breakfast." He said, "Someone must have schooled you." I said, "Nope, I've just flown in helicopter before." Master Sergeant Lacy said, "Way to go, Staff Sergeant." I said, Hoooah, Master Sergeant."

Word came down from brigade the battalion was redeploying back to Fort Hood for deactivation. It was my section's responsibility to make sure and request redeployment orders on the elements and personnel to depart country.

The morning of, Sergeant Major Brown called me in his office. He said, "Sergeant Acoma, this element of the battalion is redeploying back to Fort Hood. As you know, we were in the process of deactivation when we got deployed. Now that our mission here is complete, we have a few things to do and then we will be redeploying back before the main body does. Wheels up for this battalion PAC, is in two weeks.

Now that leaves you." You have a choice and it's not something you need to decide on immediately, but you have only a few days. You can either redeploy back to Sixth Army headquarters, or you can transfer to a unit here, which currently has a sustainment mission, that unit would probably be the 702nd Transportation Battalion. They have a PAC section that could use your expertise. You have been a great asset to this battalion and division and I felt we owed you that opportunity to make your own choice.

You've been here about four months. Most of us have been here nine months and we've families to get back to. I'm pretty sure you do also. I'm giving you two days to make a decision and get back with me, otherwise you'll be redeploying with the battalion."

I said, thank you Sergeant Major and got up to leave. He said "Oh, by the way if you want to check that unit out, it's over in Dammam Port. I can do you a strip map, to get there. You can check out one of the vehicles." I said, "Hooooah, Sergeant Major."

CHAPTER

Fifteen

I found my way over to Dammam Port. It was located near the water. The battalion was just outside the port security check, in a two story structure. I pulled into the parking lot and went to the battalion headquarters. I asked to speak to the battalion Sergeant Major. He said he was expecting me.

He told me to come in and have a seat. He said, "I've heard a lot of good things about you, I would love to have you in the battalion, but we already have a Staff Sergeant Redeployment NCOIC, but we do need Convoy Commanders and Company clerks, you have too much rank to be a clerk." He asked, "Did I have a military driver's license? I told him, I have my stateside on me, but not an in country military one."

He said, "Not a problem, that's an easy fix, what I want you to do, is go over to the truck companies. There's a First Sergeant Rock, he's B Company's First Sergeant, 1Lt Nichols is the commander. I'll give him a call and let him know you're on your way. He needs drivers and he'll get you set up." I said, "Thank you, Sergeant Major."

I found my way over to the Truck Company. When I pulled up First Sergeant Rock and his clerk SPC Jacob were sitting outside their orderly room. I said, must be nice.

First Sergeant said, "Come on in we were just looking for you." I said, "Hooooah, First Sergeant." He asked, "So, you want to be a Convoy Commander?" I said, "I don't know what a Convoy

Commander is or does." He said, "It's an easy job. You saw all those vehicles coming down the highway and lined up on the side of the road." I said, "Yes, First Sergeant."

He said, "Your job is to get them to their destination, without losing your payload. Payload is what you are carrying. You will be dealing with a lot of foreign nationalist drivers. You will not be out there by yourself. You will have Army MPs as your escort and protections. You will have to carry a firearm, an M16A1 and a 9mm pistol.

You will have a shotgun driver who will be your right hand. As a female, you need to have a male with you all the time you have to deal with a Saudi or any member of the Islamic belief. You will be the only female convoy commander in this battalion. You understand Saudis they do not speak directly to any female." I said, "That's a Roger, First Sergeant."

Now your payload will include a lot of different type of cargoes; mostly ammunitions, ordnance or bombs, and some hash and trash for the soldiers' mess hall, and field PX. Most are in large containers. Each convoy will have what we call "Bobcats". They are the Cabs that pulls the flatbeds or CONEXs. The Bobcat is used on every convoy in case of a break down.

Ammunition and ordnance are usually the heaviest cargoes. The vehicles are not our vehicles on all missions, so they are subject to break down; that's when your bobcat comes in handy. If you are carrying any kind of ammo in your cargoes, it is subject to highjack. But don't worry your MP escort are all expert shooters.

They have an NCOIC on all convoy. You are their Commander, once on that highway. Your MP's main responsibility is to direct traffic in the intersection and monitor the convoy flow on the highway. If there is a breakdown the drivers do not get paid for their payload. The MP will halt the convoy to assess the problem. If the problem cannot be fixed, the payload is dropped, and the rear bobcat will upload it and continue to take the load in on the convoy.

All convoys are monitored from the time they leave their pick up point to the drop off point at Dammam's Port. Your mission ends once all convoy vehicles are accounted for at Portside. There are usually thirty to forty vehicles per convoy, but with this push to get that ammo and equipment out of the desert, and the Saudi wants us out of their country, your convoys may double or triple in vehicles.

So for every thirty vehicles, you will have an MP escort and shooter. That's two per vehicle. They will block all intersection crossing, beginning with your vehicle the lead vehicle. All vehicles follow your command. Any accident will be called in immediately to the dispatch, and the Saudi Police handles civilian or Host Nation's incidents. Keep in mind, if a Saudi is killed in an accident, they will demand immediate restitution.

Sergeant Acoma, we need to get you over on the range to qualify you, on the M9 side arm. All commanders carry a M9, 9mm pistol. This is for your safety. You must qualify on that weapon. Most likely you may never have to use it, but it never hurts to be prepared." I said, "Hoooah, First Sergeant."

"So, SSG Acoma, when can we expect you to sign into the company?" I replied, "When 2nd Armor Division releases me." He added, "You know you will be living out your vehicle about half the time. The other time, you'll be sleeping trying to catch up on that rest.

All 702nd personnel have quarters here on the barge at the port. When you are at KKMC you will be staying in the trailers at the HHC, they have a female First Sergeant and she's very tough on those foreign nationals up there. Let me know so I can get you scheduled over at the range. SPC Jacobs will take care of that for you."

When I got back to the airfield, Sergeant Major Brown asked, "How things go?" "Pretty good, Sergeant Major." "You had a visitor a few minutes ago. A Sergeant First Class Taylor, she said she had some information for you. She said she'll catch you at the dining facilities." I said, "Thanks Sergeant Major, they want to know when I'll be released from the unit." He replied, "As soon as Master Sergeant Lacy can release you, and cut the transfer orders. Master Sergeant Lacy said, "I can have them ready by tomorrow." Sergeant Major said, "Outstanding.

Why don't you take the rest of the day off Sergeant Acoma, so you can get your things together?" I said, "Hooooah, Sergeant Major." "Since I'm going that way, I can drop you off at your quarters. You come in tomorrow with the rest of the people to get your orders. We'll get you back to your new unit." I said, "Thanks."

When I got back to the quarters, there was a note on my door from Sergeant First Class Taylor. She said, "I've got a surprise for you come by my office." I went by her office expecting to see Command Sergeant Major Howard, but instead she had a bigger surprise. She handed me a piece of paper.

It was my promotion orders. She said, "Congratulations Sergeant First Class." I was so happy. I said, "Damn. Does 2nd AD know yet?" "No, I was going to fax them a copy." "Don't, my orders are effective tomorrow. Send it to 702d Tran Bn. I just got transferred, to the 702nd Transportation Battalion as a Convoy Commander."

She said, "You what? Damn girlfriend, you're going out on that highway." I said, "I didn't have a choice either that, or redeploy back to Presidio." She asked, "You know your boy is on his way back? They left this morning. He should be pulling in here any moment now. See, its right here on the board. What units are moving forward or redeploying to the rear, the Commander and the Command Sergeant Major. Maybe you can get him to pin your strips on, Sergeant First Class."

I asked, "When you going to eat?" She said, "Right now, you hungry?" "Yeah, I've got the rest of the day off." "Oh boy, you can go in town with me. I need to pick up some things." "I've yet to see the town," I commented. "It's like being at a carnival. Since its Friday they have open market sentencing." I asked, "What's that? That sounds kind of horrific." "You'll see, it is horrific, they cut off people's hands, heads, arms and legs depending on what the crime is and the sentence."

I said, "And you stand there and watch it." "Yeah, if I don't get run off by the MPs. The Saudi Police Officers (SPOs) don't care they want us to watch." "Jackie, you have got to be kidding." "No, I'm not you'll see. Come on, I can't go in town by myself, we have to have a buddy with us." "Alright, but I'm not going to stand there and watch people being mutilated."

We walked over to the dining facility. Just as we turned the corner, there he was standing across the road clearing his side arm inside a drum barrel's hole. As we walked up Jackie said, "Command Sergeant Major Howard, you must have just pulled in." He turned and looked at us and said, "Well if it ain't my two favorite soldiers.

Yeah, I just thought I might grab some real chow before my crew rolled in. They're about two hours out." He glanced at me and said, "It's going to be a long night.

You ladies ate yet?" Jackie said, "That's where we're headed." I hadn't said a word. I was so shocked to see him. He was so dusty and dirty. He had dust everywhere, all over his face and except for around his eyes where he had taken off his goggles and placed them on his head gear.

He then said, "Staff Sergeant Acoma, you're mighty quiet. How you been?" "Pretty good, Command Sergeant Major." We walked over to the wash area where he cupped his hand together full of water and splashed it on his face and dried it with some dry paper towels.

He said, "That felt better." He then washed his hands and dried them and said, "Let's get some chow, I'm starved." He slung his M16 over his shoulder and we walked in the chow hall. He walked up to the servers and asked, "What's good?" The KP said, "Everything, Command Sergeant Major."

He said, "Outstanding." I said to myself, he's living the role. He is having fun. He ended up not getting much to eat. He grabbed a salad and some juice. He was not a coffee drinker. He asked, "Where you Sergeants sitting?" We said, "Anywhere."

Jackie asked, "So, CSM, "How was it?" He said, "It wasn't bad, wasn't bad at all. The air strike did most of the work. They cleared the way so we could do our job. I lost a couple of men to friendly fire by the RA.

It got a little chaotic on the night we had that bad dust storm; where you Sergeants headed when you leave here?" Jackie said, "I'm going to get my vehicle, so we can go do some shopping." He said, "That's just up somebody I know, alley."

I said, "No, I haven't been shopping, since I've been here." He said, "See, guilty." I said, "But I haven't, I've been working." He said, "Ok, Staff Sergeant I hear you." Jackie intoned, "She's not a Staff Sergeant too much longer; she got her orders today." He whispered and said, "My babe's a Sergeant First Class." He asked, "So when's the ceremony?" I said, I don't know, I've been waiting for you." We all started getting up. He said, "We'll talk about it."

Jackie said, "I'm going to get my vehicle and I'll meet you at your quarters. I said, "Ok." He said, "So when did all this take place. I asked, "Today, but it's not effective until tomorrow. My unit is redeploying in two weeks back to Hood, and I'm getting transferred."

He said, "Transferred, I thought you said your unit was redeploying back to Hood." They are, but I'm not going with them. He said, "When you decided on this." "Just a few hours ago." "A few hours ago, I was almost here then. Babe, babe, couldn't you have waited a day or two. We're out of here in another month. I've got to go. We'll talk about it later." He walked away, shaking his head.

I sat there on the barriers waiting for Jackie to get back. I didn't know what to think. I heard a vehicle drive up, I thought it was Jackie. It was Daniel and his driver. He got out his vehicle, told his driver to circle the block and come back. He walked over to me sitting down. I stood up.

He put his hands on his hips and said, "Staff Sergeant Acoma, what the hell made you make a decision like that." I whispered, and said, Staff Sergeant." He then said, "Val, what made you make that decision to stay here, Sergeant!"

"You did, I didn't know when you were coming back or redeploying." He took a deep breath and asked, "What unit you going to." I told him, "702nd Trans Battalion, Dammam Port." He then said, "That's all I want to know, we'll talk about it later."

His driver pulled up, he walked around and got in the vehicle. He hit the outside of his door twice and his driver pulled off. His driver asked where to Command Sergeant Major. I didn't hear the response.

Jackie pulled up and asked, "You ready?" "Yeah" She asked, "Is everything alright?" Somewhat upset, I said, "Jackie, he treated me like a private, he called me sergeant and demanded information out of me." She asked, "Well, what brought that on?" "I told him I was transferring and staying here." She then said, "So what did he say?"

"He-was-pissed; I've never seen him like that." She said, "Well he's got to have a reason." "He's redeploying in a month." "Oh, so that's the rest of the story." "I guess." He left and said we'll talk about it."

Jackie said, "Come on Val, that man loves you. He wasn't trying to hurt you. You saw how happy he was when he saw you." "I know but, he was really mean to me, you should have seen him.

He was acting like a damn, Command Sergeant Major. I thought he was going to put me at parade rest." "I would have loved seen that." I said, Jackie, "Go to shit!"

She said, "Y'all will make up, I hope before your promotion ceremony." "He might not even come, he was so mad when he left."

When we got to downtown Khobar, it was really crowded. There was a lot of military walking around shopping. There was a sign posted in reference to the sentencing. Jackie said, "I don't know what the sign said, but, let's follow the crowd." We followed the crowd over to an area that looked like an open area market for the sentencing.

There were MPs shooing all military personnel. One MP said, "Sergeant First Class, you don't want to stand there and look at this. This stuff is horrific." Jackie said, "I do." I said, "I can't watch this." She said, "Stand over there, like you looking in the jewelry store window."

I went and stared in the window. Jackie said, "That-was-gross, they cut off that man's hand." I said, "I didn't hear no body yelling." She said," "They can't, it'll put shame on their family."

She said, "They got two more. I don't know what they did, but that was enough for me." "Me too, let's go." We started going in stores. Jackie was haggling for lower prices. I was just looking at the gold. Jackie said, "This ain't like that stuff you find in the swap meets. This is real Saudi Arabian gold. It does not tarnish or turn your skin green." I said, "It's too bad I don't have a thing for gold."

We walked around until it got dark. Some of the shops started to close. Jackie said, "We need to head back." We started back and she dropped me off at my quarters.

When I got back, Staff Sergeant Mason said, "A Command Sergeant Major came by and asked me to put this note on your bed." I said, "Thanks," I read the note, it said, "Staff Sergeant (P) Acoma, I need to speak with you tomorrow, meet me at breakfast at 06:00, Command Sergeant Major Howard." I thought, "He's still treating me like a subordinate to him."

I couldn't sleep the whole night. I kept thinking about the incident between Daniel and me. I kept telling myself he was out of line. I then realized, maybe, he wasn't out of line. I took him for granted after all he is a Command Sergeant Major. Not just my boyfriend or the man I love. I just never saw him like this before and towards me.

I looked at my clock it was about 4:00 A.M. I got up took a hot shower in the hard water. I got dressed and walked out doors and sat in the same place we had our falling out. I then got up and walked over to the chow hall about 5:45. When I got there Command Sergeant Major Howard was sitting in his vehicle in the parking lot. He said, "Get in, what I have to say, I don't want anyone around."

We rode out the complex about a couple of miles down the highway and he then pulled off in the sand. He turned the vehicle off, placed both elbows on the steering wheel with his fingers interlocking together.

He then turned his head looking at me sideways and said, "Val, I love you so much, you just don't have any idea, what it does to me. All the time I was up north, all I could think about is how safe you were. I had over 2,000 soldiers under my command and all I could think of, was she safe.

There was a lot of intelligence about SCUDs and one in particular about it hitting the National Guard's Barracks on the airfield. That really got my heart racing, until I found out it was a unit from the east coast. All I'm saying babe, I worried about you all the time I was up on that border.

When we got word of a cease fire, I knew we were headed back south. I could see my babe. I told my commander I was going to be the lead on this convoy so when they get back I'll have everything set up for them when they rolled in.

When I got here yesterday, I was the happiest man in the world when I saw you and Jackie coming down the street. It took a hell of a lot for me not to grab hold of you. Now all I want to do is grab hold of you and shake some sense in your head."

He then hesitated and said, "Why Val, why couldn't you had just waited; waited until I got back from up north. If your unit had redeployed that would have been no problem. You would have gone back to Presidio, out of harm's way.

I would have followed in another month or so. Now you going to a unit that has a hell of a mission, and you don't even like to drive. You are going to be out there on that highway, pushing thousands of tons of ammunition, ordnance and artillery down a very dangerous road.

You've never done anything like this before, plus you are a female. The only female out there with all those damn foreign nationalist from who knows where or what kind of religious beliefs."

He rested his head back against his seat and said, "I don't know Val, I just don't know, what to say except to tell you," he then sat up with tears beginning to well in his eyes, raising the tone in his voice and pointed his finger at me and said, "You be careful, Sergeant First Class Valeria B. Acoma, you be very damn careful. Don't you trust anybody except your MPs and your shotgun driver".

He then said, "There are a lot of pirates out on that road and they are looking for a weakness in a convoy. You get on that highway you tell those MPs don't stop until you get to that rest stop, after that rest stop you don't stop until you reach that port." Those words stuck with me on every convoy I ran.

He then opened the door on his side of the vehicle. He got out and walked around the front to my side. He then opened my door and said, "Come here I want to show you something." I was ready to get out, to stretch my legs, after listening to that one sided conversation.

The sun was just rising up from the heated desert with its orange face. He caught my hand and then placed his hands on my shoulder and walked me to the front of his vehicle. He stood in his usual place behind me and wrapped his arms around my shoulders.

He said, "When I was up north, I made sure I got up early every morning to look out at that sunrise. I would think of you and tell it good morning." He turned me around facing him and kissed me and said "Good Morning Sunshine" and I said "Good Morning my darling".

He then asked, "Are we straight?" "We straight." He then spanked me on my behind. We stood and watched the sunrise for a moment. He then asked, "Are you hungry?" "Just a little." We drove back and ate breakfast together.

Later that day, I passed my weapons qualification on my 9mm pistol. Jackie and Daniel attended my promotion at the company, they both pinned my Sergeant First Class stripes on me. One week later I was on my very first convoy with my trainer.

My first mission carried me past the burning oil fields, of Kuwait; that was a nightmare in its self. Several times we had to get out of our vehicles and wipe our windshield to keep the black oily residue off the windows so we could see where we were driving. Night goggles and kerchiefs didn't help. That oily residue stayed in your uniforms. I had to DX or turn those uniforms in for new ones.

Just as we came out of those oil fields we came to a clear area that had an ungodly smell. It was the smell of dead flesh, burnt flesh. It was the north end of highway 80 called, "the Death highway". All you could see was charred bodies and body parts scattered all over the sides of the highway and bodies burnt and melted into the metal frame of vehicles. The stench was horrendously sickening. It was a smell I would never forget.

Master Sergeant Jenkins, my trainer said, "Sergeant First Class, I brought you through that so you can see the down side of the war we just went through. That was a convoy trying to make it back to Bagdad. But didn't because our Coalition Forces put a halt, but not before they did damage to the oil field we drove through before death highway, so as a warning always protect your payload. A lot of people's lives depend on it. If it ever gets taken, this could be the end result for all of us in the rear."

Daniel and I got to spend a lot of time before he redeployed. He decided to be the rear party on his redeployment. He stayed back to make sure his injured soldiers were medivac back to the states. That gave him some time to spend with me. Although there were no personal time we could really spend together, but, we made up for what we saw as very valuable time together.

When I went on that first solo convoy from KKMC to Damman Port; I was so nervous about the road pirates that I didn't drink hardly any water, for the whole twelve hours trip. The temperature was about 120 degrees. The next day, when I saw Daniel, I had very bad stomach cramps and backache.

I couldn't hold anything down on my stomach. Daniel asked me, "Have you been drinking water on the road?" I replied, "Not really." He indicated that, "Sounds like you're dehydrated. I know those familiar symptoms.

I think you need to go on "sick call". Why weren't you drinking your water?" he asked. I told him, "I didn't want to have to stop and "pee", in case there might be road pirates." He shook he head and said, "You got to be kidding, you got your MPs.

It doesn't take you that long to piss. Val, drink your water like I told you. Your MPs will have your back, that's what they're there for, just don't drink a lot." I said, "Okay." I really didn't want to listen to that. I was in too much pain at that time.

Daniel took me on sick call and I had to get a "Saline drip" by IV. I told Daniel, "I **hated** needles." His reply was, "Well, I bet you'll drink a lot of water, now." "Sure you right." After that, every time when we were together after a turn around on my convoy, he would always ask, have I been drinking my water?

We would take rides out to the desert and watch the sunset and we would meet before breakfast on my down time after dropping a payload off and go watch the sunrise. He was always concerned about my mission. He would meet me at the barge after a mission.

My Forbidden Love

He said, "In all our time we spent together here and once in San Francisco, we never really went shopping together. So on this particular occasion, he thought we should do a little shopping in Khobar.

I asked, "Are they doing any mutilation sentencing?" He said, "No, only on Fridays, how you know about them?" "Jackie and I came down one Friday to shop." I was glad it wasn't on a Friday because I couldn't stand to take another mutilation sentencing.

"You watched?" "No, way, but Jackie did. I couldn't take it. I went and looked in the shop windows. Some man got his hand chopped off." "Well, you don't have to worry about that today."

Daniel and I went looking in some of the jewelry stores while in Khobar. He commented, "You know, I've never bought you a gift, even when we were cohabiting in San Francisco. I want to buy you something, that'll make you always remember me."

Pick something out, something you can always wear and not hide like a gold chain." I said, "Ooh, no not the Bling, Bling." "What about a ring, I see you're still not wearing one?" "That's a good thought. Whenever I touch it or look at it I'll always think of you." So we looked at several rings.

I noticed a small dainty ring, one made like an oblong four sided figure. I asked, "What it's called?" The jeweler said, "It's called an "Eternal Slave Ring". It's a 25 carat real gold, and would not ever tarnish. Arabian women wear them on their toes and finger for life." I said, "That's it, I want that, how much?" The jeweler gave some number in Riyal which ended up costing about $200 American dollars.

Daniel managed to haggle him down to about 375 riyal or $100. I got my "eternal slave ring". He then said, "Now your love is eternally mine." "And I'm eternally indebted to you. Now I must buy you one." "I already have a wedding band." I said, "A birth stone ring, when is your birthday?" He said, "July, that's great, we both have Ruby as our birthstone."

I asked the jeweler to show us Rubies. We found one, a beautiful ruby for about the same price and we bought it together. He said, "I will always wear it on my right ring finger."

I put mine on my right ring finger. (I still wear that ring, I have never taken it off. It's been over twenty years. Whenever I touch it or turn it on my finger I think of him and the last words he said before our last good-bye) "I will always remember you as my wife, for that three week fling, in San Francisco; but now, you're my Saudi bride."

We watched our final sunset on his jeep together over the Arabian Desert horizon, as it slipped below the Desert sand. He left the next week for redeployment and I continued my mission as a Convoy Commander. That was the last time I saw him. I kept my self very busy doing convoys. Subsequently, I got caught up in doing missions.

I try not to think about him, but every time I looked at my hand, I felt his presence. I felt this time I had lost him forever. There were some times I wanted to cry, and sometimes I did. We had no means of communicating.

Jackie left a couple of months later. She was offered a really good position with the United Nations, and said, she was going in the Inactive Ready Reserves (IRR). She said, "This is an opportunity I could not refuse. Val, you should come on and work there."

I said, "No, I do not like New York and I still have some unfinished business back in California." She asked, "Christen" "No, not really." She then said, "Oh, Daniel." I said "Yeah." She asked, "Have you heard from him?" I said, "No, not even a letter." She said, "I know he loves you. He told me."

I said, "I'm going to be alright. I can keep busy. I might extend until the mission is complete." I asked when she's leaving. She said, "In about three days." "I'll be up north by then." She motioned, "Come on girlfriend, give me a big hug." I thought to myself *I am all by myself now, for sure.*

Maybe, I do need to go home. But I didn't, I ran convoys for about three more months. I told Jackie I'll call her when I get back in the states. I might take her up on that job. We said our good byes with a lot of tears. I didn't see her for about five years.

One of my most serious convoy was on the push south. It was one of those times, where I had to make a decision I was worried after I made it. I had a crazy Saudi, driving fast coming up behind one of

My Forbidden Love

my convoys, weaving in and out around my vehicles. I saw him in my rear view mirror about a mile back. SPC Diggs, my shotgun driver was driving, told me, Sergeant First Class, we got trouble, that driver is going to kill somebody or get killed.

There was another vehicle coming towards us in a white fast moving car. I thought to myself, I hope that fool behind us don't try to pass these other vehicles. My payload was all ammunition some smart bombs in the rear, for safety purpose. That fool darted, out behind one of my vehicles and tried to make a go for more than one vehicle. The oncoming car passed us, flying.

The fool darted back in and the vehicle behind him jammed him into the vehicle in front. It smashed him between two eighteen wheelers; killed him instantly. The oncoming car never stopped, it kept going.

I had my driver pull over and I radioed there was a serious accident and a possible fatality. I then went back to where the accident happened. I told the MPs to pass the word that all drivers should stay inside their vehicles.

Staff Sergeant Simmons, a very cute boyish looking white guy, was the MPs team NCOIC. He said, "Sergeant First Class, you got big trouble." I demanded, "Give it to me straight SGT, what's up?" He explained, "You've got one dead Saudi, bad business; if a Saudi dies, the one who caused the accident will die also. That's probably why that oncoming driver, who caused the accident, didn't stop because he knew it was his fault. But in reality it wasn't his fault although he was going over 100 miles an hour.

Now, you got a scared shitless irate Pakistani, in that vehicle, who believes he is going to die, when the Saudi authority shows up and he might or will die, because the Saudi Police Officers (SPO) don't play. They have the authority to kill on the spot. I've seen it happen. They are the judge, jury and executioner at traffic fatalities."

He then advised, "Sergeant First Class, you have a choice. Most of these drivers are Foreign Nationalist, with families back in their countries. Now, as I see it; it's our responsibility to protect these drivers when we are on the road. You, Sergeant First Class, is the Commander, on this road, it's your call.

We can drop the load and bobcat it, and continue on our mission and have the other bobcat drive that driver to the Iranian border, which is only few hours east of the Kuwaiti border. You, SFC, need to make a decision, quick. You know how those Saudi drive; they'll be here in the next hour."

I said, "Ok, Staff Sergeant Simmons, here's what we're going to do. Radio your guys in the rear to bring up those two bobcats. Drop that load now! So when the other one get up here, we'll up load it. It's supposed to take five minutes I want it done in three. We need to be on the road in two minutes, after that up load.

Get that, irate Pakistani and his cab, off my convoy now. Get that other bobcat driver to put him in his cab and get him and his cab the hell out of here. In the meanwhile, you stay back and talk to the SPO when they arrive, because you know they will not talk to me.

So, with that in mind I'm about to pull this convoy out and head south." I asked with concern, "Are you gonna be alright?" He said, "I'm good Sergeant First Class. I've been through this before." "See you at the Rest Stop." "Hoooah, Sergeant First Class."

I looked through my side view mirror and the bobcat with the irate Pakistani and his cab hooked to the back of his bobcat was out of sight heading northwest on highway 80. Once it got to KKMC, it should be headed east toward Iranian-Pakistani borders.

We passed the SPOs about 45 minutes down the highway. I thought to myself good timing, damn good timing. By the time they get to the accident, that bobcat should be heading east.

We waited for Staff Sergeant Simmons to catch up at the Rest Stop. We were there about an hour when Simmons pulled in. I said "That was quick what happened?" He said, "I told them what had happened, that an Iraqi Kurdish driver caused the accident.

They didn't want to finish the report they left heading northwest flying." I reminded him, "I thought you said that guy was Pakistani." He said, "I don't know, they all look the same to me." I smiled and shook my head and said, "Outstanding, Staff Sergeant." He said,

My Forbidden Love

"Hoooah, Sergeant First Class, I'll pull that rear bobcat off line, and cover the rear."

I said, "Hoooah, Staff Sergeant, see you on the bottom." (End of the trail).When we got to the company, First Sergeant had Staff Sergeant and I, make sure the accident report coincided. He said, "If the information has any flaws, the US is liable for the civilian's life, and required to pay restitution to the victim's family. Most likely that will happen anyway. United States wants to keep Saudi as an Allie.

Three weeks later, I had another load coming out of KKMC. Who did I see in the driver's yard, were none other than my irate Pakistani; he was sitting on his rollup bed with his buddies smoking a water pipe and drinking their Pakistani coffee. He had to have been high, they don't usually talk to women. They were calling "Hey big SARG", I smiled and kept walking.

I asked, "First Sergeant Duarte, "What is he doing here, I thought he went to Pakistan." She said, "He might've not left, they do that shit all the time. They have accidents, vehicles breakdown and they come back up here get a vehicle and go out on the next convoy." "Don't put him on my convoys."

She said, "I'll tell Jack, the yard chief. You better watch him; he likes you. You saved his life." "No, I didn't!" She said, "Yes you did Sergeant First Class. The Saudis were going to kill him, right there in front of you and your whole damn convoy. They would make an example for you, and that convoy would never forget. They would have chopped his head off."

She continued, "Just don't go out there in that yard by yourself, they might steal you and take you to Pakistan. You know they got a white slavery ring coming out of these driver's yards. That's why I have a guard around your trailer when you do an overnight." I said, "You lying." She said, "Yeah, I'm lying, but you bet not go out in that yard by yourself. They'll steal you and take you across that border, it's only two hours away, and sell you on the white slavery market."

I said, "You don't have to tell me more than once, I'm going to check my payload inventory (was heavy artillery, ammunition and ordnance, damn I hated that type of inventory it is a road pirate's dream)."

My manifest included ninety-five vehicles a triple load and no Pakistani drivers on the driver's roster. I was ready to roll out at 06:00 in the morning. I plan to be at Dammam's Port by 18:00 tomorrow night.

First Sergeant said, "Alright Sergeant First Class, I won't be here when you roll-out, but you be careful on that road. I said, "I will and I see you First Sergeant, on the next upside. We rolled out at 06:00 the next morning.

On my last convoy, I rolled into Dammam port with about 100 vehicles with nothing but heavy artillery and equipment. I had put in my paper for extension. The mission was far from completion. The Ammo Supply Depot was still filled with ammunition that needed to come south.

When I got back to the Company, First Sergeant Rock asked me to come see him. He asked me to close the door when I came in. He asked, "You requested an extension?" I said, "Yes, I did First Sergeant." He said, "I'm not going to approve it." I said, "Can I ask why?" He said, "Sure, "I'll be more than happy to tell you why."

He continued, "When you came to the unit back in March or April, when we first got that mission to push that ammo from up north. There was a Command Sergeant Major Howard, who came by here about you. He looked like he just came out of the desert. He was mad as hell. Still dusty and dirty, he asked me to revoke your transfer orders.

I told him I couldn't, I had a very critical mission to get all that ammo and ordnance out of the desert by a certain time, or else we would have to leave it for the Saudi. Department of Defense (DOD) doesn't want to do that." He said, "Ok, I'm going to ask you for a favor, Senior NCO to Senior NCO; brother in arms to brother in arms. If the mission is not completed by the end of her orders, don't let her extend. Send her home."

First Sergeant said, "I asked him what you are to him?" He told me, "To be perfectly honest with you First Sergeant, I'm in love with her. She's here because of me and I'm on my way home, but now she has to stay, because she didn't know when I was leaving.

He said, don't get me wrong but, she's a hell of a soldier, she'll complete her mission; but she's also, head strong, impulsive and hard headed. "Top" I love her and I plan to spend the rest of my life with her. Just send her back to the states when her time is up. We've been through too much together, then to lose her over here?"

First Sergeant said, "I told him I can only imagine him a Command Sergeant Major, and you as a Staff Sergeant at that time. I told him, I'll look out for you, after all she'll be the only female convoy commander out there on that road; and I'll send her home when her mission is over.

Sergeant Acoma I'm sorry, I made that promise to Command Sergeant Major Howard and I'm bound to keep that promise; as a First Sergeant to a Command Sergeant Major. I hope you understand that.

Oh by the way, that fatality accident about three months ago. The Saudi are still trying to stick that on someone. Staff Sergeant Simmons has redeployed. I get you out of here it'll be all over with. So, the way I see, it's high time for you to leave." I concurred, "Maybe it's time for me to go, First Sergeant." He said, "It is Sergeant First Class, it is.

Look at it this way you help put a hell of a dent in that PUSH. You ran 26 convoys to this day, and transported over 150 thousand tons of ammo and ordnance back to the states. That's a hell of a job Sergeant First Class."

He then asked, "When you want to get out of here?" I replied, "As soon as you cut the order." "I'll talk to the Battalion Sergeant Major." "Hoooah, First Sergeant." We shook hands, he then said, "Take care of that Command Sergeant Major; he loves you very much." I replied, "Thanks First Sergeant," and left for the day.

I redeployed on New Year's Eve at 11:00 p.m. We went through three time zones that celebrated New Year's Eve, because we were going back through time. I got to Fort Dix on December the 31st at 9:00 in the evening.

I was really suffering from Jet Lag. We had to go through custom and then given sleeping quarters for the night. Some stayed up to celebrate New Year. I was too tired. I went to bed. The next day I had reservation to fly into San Francisco.

I got home to my place, I had been gone for almost six days short of a year. My apartment seems the same. I called Christen to let him know I was back in San Francisco. I was surprised he was answering his phone. I told him I was home in San Francisco. I had to come to LA in a few days after I get some rest to in process back in the unit.

I then tried to call Daniel. When I heard his voice I hung up. I was not sure what to say to him. I decided, I'll call him tomorrow.

I slept for about three days and fooled around the apartment. I went by Sixth Army DCST, Command Sergeant Major Douglas was still there. He was in the hall when I came in. He said, "Sergeant First Class, welcome back, come on in. "Congratulations on the promotion it's definitely well deserved." I said, "Thanks CSM." "See I told you, you'll get it." "You sure did CSM."

He asked, "You headed back to the Support Command?" "Yes, Command Sergeant Major." He added, "There's going to be a big celebration in DC, in about two weeks." I can get orders cut for you to participate in it, as a representative from Sixth Army."

I said, "That'll be great CSM, I'll like that." "Great I'll put you on the list, tomorrow there will be a representative from the Recruiting Command looking for recruiters for the RA and Army reserves. You're a hero, you'll make a great recruiter." I said, "Hero, I'm no hero."

He informed me, "I heard about you on those convoys; only female moving ammunition and ordnance on the PUSH south. You did a hell of a job." "I guess so." How many convoys, Sergeant First Class?" I said, "Ooh about 26." "What's your numbers?" "About 150 thousand tons, I'm told, I wasn't keeping track I was just doing my missions," I said." "That's a hell of lot of ammunition and ordnance; and a mission accomplishment, Sergeant First Class.

You should show up tomorrow for that recruiting "Recruit the Recruiter" you're a hero, you may be what they're looking for." As he leaned forward in his chair and continued, "Sergeant First Class, there're good soldiers and there are very good soldiers.

Then there are heroes, and it's not about whom they are, it's about what they've done. No one may ever tell you that but, you're a hero. So go get 'em hero. I smiled and said, "Hoooah, Command Sergeant Major."

He then asked, "You heard from your buddy, Command Sergeant Major Howard?" "No not really." "Well, you know he's an instructor at the Sergeant Major's Academy. He's got about three months left on his tour." "Tell him hi, if you talk to him, again." "You still living here, same place same number." "Yes, Command Sergeant Major."

"I'll give you a call, when I get those orders cut." "Hoooah, Command Sergeant Major. I got some things to do." He reminded me, "Don't forget about tomorrow and wear your Deserts." I said, "I'll be there and thanks again, CSM."

I went to the Whole Foods to pick up a few groceries. I got a bottle of Mateus, sharp cheese and strawberries. I was walking in the door when I heard the phone. I thought maybe it's, Christen.

I picked up the phone and it was Daniel's voice. My heart sunk like a torpedo. He said, "Hey babe, I see you made it back." I said, "Hey honey." He asked, "You called me a few days back?" "I did, but I hung up." "Well, welcome back, to the real world; so what you going to do now?" "Catch up on some rest. Go home to Virginia and see family. I have to go to LA and check back in my unit.

I went by DCST and talked to your buddy Command Sergeant Major Douglas. He told me y'all been talking." He said, "Yeah, "We've been communicating." "He asked me to go to DC, to participate in the Welcome Home Parade." "You going go?" I replied, "Yeah, it's close to home and it might be fun plus, I'll get paid for it." "That should be nice.

I missed you babe." "I missed you too, honey." He asked, "You still wearing our ring." "All the time, I've never taken it off, even when I shower, and you." He said, "All the time and I've never taken it off.

When you get time and all rested up, why don't you come down and spend some time with me." I said, "That sound like a plan. I'll let you know." He said, "The trip's on me."

I said, "I beat you can't guess what I'm about to do?" He said, "You've got some Mateus, strawberries and Cheese." I said, "Yes, I got some Kenney G, and Frankie Beverly and Maze. I'm going to sit here and think about the last time you and I were together.

I hesitated a little and asked, "Daniel what's wrong?" He answered, "Nothing, why?" "Because, we've been talking for five minutes, and you have not once said, I love you. Usually by now you would have said it at least three times." He said, "No, I was just wondering the same thing about you. You haven't once said I love you." "I was waiting for you."

"Come on babe, that's not like us. I thought we had a solid loving relationship." I asked, "Well what happened?" He said, "I don't know, you tell me." I said, "All I know is when you left Saudi, I didn't hear from you, until you called me a few minutes ago. Tell me Daniel, was it something I did, the convoys. I had a commitment that I couldn't get out of. You know this, because I know you talked to First Sergeant Rock."

He asked, "Are you mad?" "Not any more. That goes to show, you're a Command Sergeant Major, who has a lot of damn power. You've proven that. I'm not mad just astonished, at what you're capable of doing and getting it accomplished, just because you are a Command Sergeant Major."

Very sternly he said, "Val, that's what Command Sergeant Majors do. They throw their rank and power around to get what they want and take care of their soldiers. They usually get it. I didn't get what I wanted, so I settled for the next best thing." "And just what was that Daniel J. Howard, Command Sergeant Major?" I asked sarcastily.

He slightly raised his tone and said, "I got them to not, extend your orders. I wanted them to revoke them but they couldn't because it was a Department of Defense (DOD) mission. I would have taken it to the Secretary of Defense, if I thought it would've made a difference."

He lowered the tone of his voice, "Val, you are the woman I fell in love with, and love. It is my responsibility to look out for you, if I think you are not doing a good job at it. Val, you are impulsive, head strong and hard headed and most of all recently, I found you to be very tenacious, but I still love you very much. And, I would do it again, if it meant keeping you safe.

This thing about you being a convoy commander, you were like a bull in a china shop. You had no idea what you were getting into. I have to give you credit, once you are committed, you are totally committed.

I heard how successful you were on your missions. I was very proud of you. But I wanted you back before your luck ran out. I could not live with myself if anything would have happened to you out on that highway. But, now you're back and you can hate me, but that's ok, because I still love you and deeply committed to that love, and you.

So, what are you doing?" "Drinking Mateus." "I thought so." "Daniel, so where do we go from here? Am I going to always be that other woman? The one you fell in love with but couldn't have. Also are you going to always be the other man waiting for me to spend time with you whenever I can? How long are we going to do this? Is that what our relationship has become? If it is, then it's not fair to either of us.

Tell me Daniel, do we continue to go on with that life we had before we met each other. While holding on to the beautiful memories and moments we shared for three weeks here in San Francisco; that extended into the Saudi Arabian desert. You see I thought about this when I was going up and down Highway 80.

I asked myself is it fair to either of us to have the illusion, that someday we will spend the rest of our days together? I could not see it in our future. So, I thought maybe it is best this way, that we have not contacted each other.

Just remember, you are what kept me going on those convoys. One day, I'll see you again, because you are that eternal flame that burns in my heart."

He commented, "Sounds like that Mateus has got you going." I said "You right." He said, "On that note, I'm going to hang up. But you let me know where you want to go from here. This time you lead and I'll follow. Good night my darling, I still love you and in love with you." I said, "I still love you and in love with you." We hung up.

The next day I went to the Recruit the recruiter program. I took a packet and was selected as a recruit recruiter. I went home on the train out of Oakland, because I wanted to see greenery, since I had been in the desert for so long. It was a three day trip. Command Sergeant Major Douglas faxed my orders to participate in the "Welcome Home Celebration" in DC. I participated in it and flew back to San Francisco.

I got selected for recruiting duty by the Army Recruiting Command. Three weeks later, Department of the Army sent me my packet and orders, having me report to Fort Ben Harrison, IN, as a recruit recruiter to the Army Recruiting Command Training Center. My life was now headed in a different direction as a soldier.

I never heard from Daniel again. I called several times during the years but hung up when I heard his sexy voice. It was hard, but I soon went on with my life. I guess he did also.

I often think of him when I touch my ring of eternal love; I still wear on my right ring finger. Years passed and I never could love the way I loved Daniel. He left a huge hole in my heart. I hope he's happy and gone on with his life; just knowing him, I know he did.

The End

Soon to be Release

Continuing Sagas

"My Forbidden Love – A Soldier's Love Story"

"Forever My Love"

"Love, Life's Eternal Promise"

"Love, Our Eternal Flame"

And

"Love, Life's Endless Destiny"

www.ingramcontent.com/pod-product-compliance
Ingram Content Group UK Ltd.
Pitfield, Milton Keynes, MK11 3LW, UK
UKHW022226230426
12048UKWH00016BA/1088